Ewald and the Gems of Time

By Ameer Idreis
Illustrated by Hanadi Bader

© 2012, Ameer Idreis
ISBN 978-1-300-14049-8

ALL RIGHTS RESERVED. This book contains material protected under International and Federal Copyright Laws and Treaties. Any unauthorized reprint or use of this material is prohibited. No part of this book may be reproduced or transmitted in any form or by any means, electronic or mechanical, including photocopying, recording, or by any information storage and retrieval system without express written permission from the author. Except of the use of brief quotations in a book review. This book is a work of fiction. Names, characters, places, and events are either a product of the author's imagination or are used fictitiously. Any resemblance to actual persons, living or dead, is entirely coincidental.

Chapter 1
Farewell

There was a light breeze, it was a warm summer day, and everyone was outside. Almost everyone had bought ice cream from the truck standing by. Everyone except for Ewald, in fact he wasn't doing anything. He was only sitting on the cream colored bench, and gazing at the old oak tree. Ewald was a very lonely twelve year-old. In school he didn't have any friends, because everyone thought he was strange and odd. The bright sun shining in his face, made his brown hair look lighter than it was, and his hazel eyes seemed to glow. The air around the meadow was fresh, and you could almost smell the beginning of the crispy fall. Only one tree stood in the whole meadow, the one Ewald felt so fascinated by, the one everybody else disregarded. The oak tree with dark green leaves, swaying in the wind.

Then, suddenly there was a loud high-pitched screech, everyone froze of surprise. Dark clouds filled the sky, and the wind started to get faster and faster by the second. People started to run to their houses, adults dragging kids from the park. Ewald jumped on his feet and ran as fast as he could, in the direction of his home. His mother warned him that this would happen someday and he should come back home as soon as possible. He actually never asked why she thought this would happen, he just nodded his head to her command.

Ewald felt tiny drops of water spraying on his hands, as he ran out of the meadow, and down a narrow and grey sidewalk. He turned down a street and there he saw his family's small 23 year-old house, the golden 27 house number shining as if it had just been polished. The outside of his house was covered

[4]

in red bricks, and his house only had a few windows. The shutters were painted an aqua blue same as it's rusty front door. Ewald knocked rapidly on the door, as if he had seen a monster behind him. Six seconds later, the front door opened slowly. An old lady with gray hair and wrinkled skin; popped her head through the small opening. She had an umbrella in her hand as if she was expecting a robber. She stared at Ewald for a couple of seconds and then finally opened her mouth, but no words came out. She signaled him into the house. Although he had never seen her before, he somehow recognized her from somewhere.

"Ewald is that you" he heard his mother say from the upper level of their home. "Yes Ma, I'm back" he replied to her looking up the stairs that stood following the front door. Then, the elderly woman pointed at the dining table. In the middle of the wooden structure was a golden colored turkey, with three plates circling around it. It seemed as thought the senior stranger was going to stay for dinner. Ewald set his black and white shoes near the small purple mat, and headed towards the table.

Just as he was going to sit on his usual metal chair, a loud thud boomed through the house. It shook the front of the house and then flew to the back, like a wave of energy. To Ewald he thought the sound was coming from the front door. Then, Ewald's mother came running down the stairs. She was wearing her reading glasses, which sat at the tip of her nose. "Ewald come with me, now" his mother commanded, while taking off the tiny pair of glasses nervously. Ewald quickly got up and followed her down the stairs to the basement, the elderly woman ran behind him. When they got to the bottom of the stairs Ewald's mother turned around and hugged him. Her warmth spread around him, covering his wet cold body. Then, she stepped back slowly and Ewald noticed tears were falling down her cheek. His mother could cry about the simplest of things, but Ewald knew by the look in her eyes that this was different, this was way more important. Her brown hair shining in the cheap lighting, made her tears almost disappear. "Good bye, Ewald" she muttered. There was a blue flash, and then everything went dark.

Chapter 2

Transported

A blurry face came into focus, a man with a short black beard and black hair was staring straight at Ewald. Ewald's vision got clearer as he opened his eyes wider. "Samantha, he's waking up," said the bearded man. The same lady from his house came around to the opposite side of the bed that Ewald was laying down in. He looked around the room; the walls were made of white bricks with cursive writing all over. A huge white chandelier hung from the twenty-foot high ceiling. "Who are you? Where am I?" Ewald seemed to be looking at the woman, as if asking her. But instead the man replied, "I'm Dr. Kyle, and this is Professor Katherine, you're at a special hospital." "Special, What do you mean special?" he asked back. "I'm sorry Ewald, I don't think I should be the one to explain this, it's complicated" the man said, he looked truly sorry. Then, both adults stepped away from Ewald's bed; the bed rotated and started moving to Ewald's right. It rolled past all the beds and went through the large white archway, which had a giant blue stone at the pointed top.

The bed was crazy; it dodged tables, chairs, and cabinets, it even passed by people, nearly hitting them. In the background Ewald heard a loud bell chime, it repeated itself three times before stopping. "Creek" the wheels screeched. The bed suddenly stopped, and Ewald would have gone flying through the air, if he hadn't hung on to the metal sidebars of the bed. Ewald looked horrified, "What kind of place is this?" he asked himself. "What a freak-show" he thought. He noticed an exit sign to his left; he jumped down from the moving bed and onto the eggshell tile floor. He was worried, he ran as fast as he could down a long hallway, "The sooner he got out, the better" he thought. But, he could not see a door; the only thing he saw was a tall, and thin girl at the end of the hallway. He stopped and began to walk, getting closer and closer. Until, he could see her face. She had long blond hair, blue eyes, and a white smile. Her clothes were somewhat boy-like, brown pants with a golden belt, a military styled sweater with a sparkly green shirt, and a plain white cap.

"So, your Ewald..." she said while looking down at a piece of parchment she held in her hand. "Ewald Ellington, could you follow me?" she asked but before getting an answer she turned around and walked to the end of the hallway. Ewald walked after her keeping his distance, as he didn't know whom she was. When the girl got to the end of the hallway, she looked back and waited for Ewald to catch up. Then, she reached into a pocket that was on the golden belt, and brought out some pink powder. She waved her hand and threw the powder on the wall. The wall moaned as the center split and opened as if it was an elevator. "Welcome to Drolers, hospital and host to the annual school selection program" the girl said "I'm Julie, by the way, Julie Sanders."

Ewald looked through the large wooden door; beds in rows were lined up. The beds had blue covers that looked like they had been used a thousand times, and white fluffy pillows that were covered in dust. About a hundred people were in this large room.

"This is where you'll be sleeping" she said, "In here?" Ewald replied. "Well, only until we find the right school for you" she answered, the parchment she was holding glowed neon green. Julie looked down at the parchment "Got to go welcome someone else, make yourself at home" She said as she walked away. Ewald stepped foot on the old wooden floor, he walked to an empty bed and sat down. He looked around, the bed to his right was empty, but the one on the left held a boy about his age, sleeping peacefully. Ewald looked at the boy closer, he had black hair and a large smile that spread across his face. It was getting late, so Ewald got under the covers and fell fast asleep. As if he was still at home sleeping in his bedroom.

Ewald stood in his basement, his mother crying, the old woman looked just as upset as his mother. His mother's orange sweater and sweet scent vanished, as the woman grabbed for a crooked stick in her back pocket. A flash of blue light emerged from the woman's hand, misery filled the air. Then, he heard something that he hadn't heard before, he remembered his mother saying "Good bye, Ewald", but he didn't remember her saying "I didn't get to explain this to him." Even thought he didn't remember it, he felt like it was real, that she actually said that sentence with her beautiful soft voice. Then,

[10]

the thought disappeared, and he found himself lying in the crazy hospital bed again, the two adults staring at him, but this time he read the writing on the wall. "Magic is not found in the object but in the heart. Those who seek power will not get it, but those who need power shall find it" what did that all mean. Is that what this whole thing is about magic and power?

Chapter 3
Dragon Eggs

"Ewald, wake up" said Julie as she shook him back and forth. Ewald opened his eyes slowly and sat in the wooden bed. "Come on Ewald" she said, Ewald got out of his bed. "Where is everyone?" Ewald asked, "They're down stairs eating breakfast, and I suggest we go eat before it's all gone" she replied. He and Julie walked out of the giant door, then, she turned around and threw some of the pink dust, and the wall slowly closed shut. Julie and Ewald walked down the shiny white stairs, which he hadn't noticed were there before. When they got to the bottom of the stairs, they turned left and they were in a huge room filled with tables. It had hundreds of people sitting down, eating, and talking. "Enjoy your breakfast" Julie said, "Where do I get it from?" he asked, "Just sit at a table" she replied, and then she walked away and back out of the room. Ewald looked for an empty table. Then, he sat down and a tray appeared out of mid-air. The green tray held a plate of blue eggs, a piece of crispy toast, and orange juice.

Ewald was about to get started on breakfast, but the black haired boy who slept on the bed to Ewald's left came and sat beside him. "Hi, I'm Alexander Egond, Alex for short" the boy said shyly, "Hello, Alex, I'm Ewald Ellington" Ewald replied. Alex forced a smile on his face. "I saw you sleep in, and thought I should say hi" Alex said, Alex sat down and a green tray appeared in front of him. Ewald looked back down at his plate of blue eggs, "These are chicken eggs, right?" Ewald asked Alex. "Well, they're dragon eggs, but they taste just the same" Alex answered. Suddenly, Ewald felt nauseous, but Alex didn't seem to mind, he was stuffing his mouth with each swallow. Ewald picked up the clear glass of orange juice and touched it to lip, sipping slowly. Unlike Alex, he was going slowly on his food.

A loud bell had rung making a few students jump. "Come on Ewald, let's go" Alex suggested while pulling Ewald's hand. "To where?" Ewald asked, "We're going back to the dorm room" he answered. They both walked towards the entrance of the eating area, turned right and up the stairs. Then, they went into the giant dorm room, and sat on the beds that they had slept on the previous night. "Listen up, there are four schools. You will be put into different schools," Julie said into the megaphone in her right hand. Julie went around to each person, each time she looked down at a small piece of parchment. "Alex, how could that piece of parchment have so much written on it?" Ewald asked Alex. "The writing on the parchment keeps changing" Alex answered. "How?" he asked, "They'll teach that at school" he said to Ewald, not really answering his question. Luckily there weren't that many people ahead of them, so they didn't have to wait that long.

Ewald was next, he heard Julie tell the girl with ginger hair that she was going to Borants. Julie came over, looked down at the parchment and read "Tralbon." What every 'Tralbon' was it sounded nice to Ewald. Julie then approached Alex, she looked down at the parchment, "Tralbon" she announced. Alex had a smile on his face, he was glad he was going to school with someone he knew, even if he only knew his name. Ewald for some reason felt happy he got into the same school as Alex, he somehow felt like they could be friends. After Julie, told everyone their schools, she went back to the front. "You'll all need to pack up by midnight, except for you Ewald, your stuff will already be there waiting" she told to the whole group.

The large clock that hung in the eating area, struck midnight. Everyone had their bags by their sides. Ewald and Alex sat together as Julie walked into the room. "Would everyone who is attending Tralbon School please follow me" she said. They both got up and followed Julie out of the room. The group of about seventy students walked passed the stairs and stopped at the wall; she reached her hand into a compartment on her belt. When she raised her hand, a couple of specks of pink powder were pinched between her fingers. She splashed it on the solid brick wall and a path emerged leading to the dark outside world.

A yellow school bus stood in the middle of the dusty road. "Hop on everyone" Julie said after she turned to the teenagers. "Can we all fit in that?" a short blond student asked while looking at the bus.

"Yes, just get on" Julie answered. After everyone got on to the crowded bus including Julie, "Get ready," a high-pitched voice said. A loud engine roared as the bus expanded in all directions, making more room. "Hang on" the same voice squeaked. Everyone quickly sat down, from the outside of the bus an 8 foot-long set of wings appeared on both sides of the bus, they were painted the same dark yellow as the rest of the bus. Then, the bus drove a couple of meters and flew off, blowing dust into the darkness.

Chapter 4
The Entrance

Ewald and Alex sat beside each other, Ewald pressing his face to the cold window of the yellow flying bus. Everything was passing by him so quickly; the past 24 hours had been crazy. He just was sitting in the park and now he was on a flying bus that was soaring between the grey clouds of the dark night. The only source of light had come from the moon, glowing white in the cold air. Then, suddenly a yellow distant light appeared, all the students in the bus stood up to see where the light was coming from. The flying bus suddenly shook, knocking everyone back to their seats. Ewald looked back out the frozen window; a structure now appeared around the glowing light. A dark brick tower surrounded by gargoyle pillars stood, it looked like an old castle far in the distance.

Alex leaned in closer to Ewald's ear, "Soon we'll get to see 'The Silver Entrance', I've never seen it, but I've heard that it's a very beautiful thing" Alex almost whispered into Ewald's ear. Ewald tried to imagine what 'The Silver Entrance' could look like but there were too many possibilities to put a visual image in his head. As they grew closer and closer to the far away structure, Julie stood up from the front of the bus and turned to face the rest of the bus. "We will arrive at the entrance in about two minutes. Please make sure you have your entire luggage when exiting the bus," said Julie towards all of the students. Then, she turned around and sat back down on the grey seat.

For the next minute and a half, Ewald sat there looking out the nearly frozen window, while Alex sat almost silently to his right. Then, Ewald noticed that the bus was slowly getting closer to the ground. He looked down at the landscape, which to his surprise was a very dark ditch, not a flat meadow as it had appeared before. After, he had pondered about the ground for about ten seconds, he returned his attention to the distant mansion, which now wasn't as far away as it had been before. A couple seconds later the bus stopped moving forward and was hovering only two inches above the cold rocky ground. Then, with a light thud, the bus landed softly and the door opened. Julie was the first one to stand up; the group of students followed her out of the bus. Chatter broke out between the students; everyone was talking about how excited they were to be there.

A student pointed towards the castle, one-by-one they began to look at where she had pointed. A giant silver gate stood in front of them, almost all the students had their mouth's open of astonishment. "Is that 'The Silver Entrance'?" a boy in the front row of students asked to no one in particular, but nobody answered. The large metal gate fascinated them all. Beyond the gate was a very organized garden. Although it did not have any sort of flowers, it did have amazing hedges, the kind you might see in a royal garden. The 15-foot high silver gate was shining with the light of the full moon. The metal that decorated the center of the gate was curved into vines and swirls; the width of each twisted bar wasn't very thick. The bars that ran around the outside of the gate and right through the middle were much more thicker than the ones in the center. Two giant walls of hedges stood beside the metal gate, stretching up to a giant tower. Suddenly, a trumpet sounded far away, hitting a low note. Then, the gate split in half and opened. Julie stepped into the pathway, and the group followed behind.

It was dark, only a couple of lanterns were floating in the air. "How are they floating in mid-air?" Ewald asked Alex, "Magic" Alex said in an excited voice. They walked past all the oddly shaped hedges. A thin layer of fog slithered on the rocky path. On each side of them, a large wall-like hedge stood nearly touching the clouds. Ahead of them sat a fountain; in the center was a statue of two lions, on their legs, back-to- back. The old beige fountain looked at least a hundred years- old. As Ewald passed by staring at the two lions, he noticed a hole in each of their open mouths'. The holes were probably where the water had come straying out from, and down to the large tub below it. Ancient symbols and letters were carved into the outside of the circle tub, where the water would have stayed. Ewald wondered what the symbols could mean. Behind the fountain was a very tall tower that was even taller than the hedges, which seemed to end there.

A dark-skinned boy came up to Ewald from the back of the group. He had messy black hair and dark brown eyes. His clothes looked worn-out; he wore baggy jeans and a dark green shirt that looked somewhat good on him. "I'm Dhiman Letap," said the boy, Ewald just nodded his head. "Do you know how to find the area of a hexagon?" asked Dhiman, Alex snickered, "Pardon me" Ewald replied. "Do you know how to find the area of a hexagon?" Dhiman repeated, "No" Ewald answered, Ewald was amused with the random question. "Oh, well maybe I can teach you sometime." Dhiman said loudly. Multiple thoughts filled Ewald's head, "Why is he asking me a math question" to "Why is he showing off?" As they walked past all the grey statues and silver armor, Ewald turned his head back to see where the fountain was now. The fountain stood far away nearly hidden by the fog, 'The Silver Entrance' standing high above the ground, was now closed, and nothing was visible behind it except for the dark black sky.

The tower was now about only 15-feet away from the group. A large arched wooden door carved into the front of the brick structure sat closed in the dark. As they stepped forward, two lanterns that hung on each side of the door, lit up with fire, and the door was more detailed than they had expected. The old brown wooden door had the name of the school written on it, in a very fancy font, 'Tralbon'. "Wow!" everyone exclaimed, everyone except for Dhiman Letap. "I've already come here once, with my father. It's not that amazing" Dhiman protested. Ewald turned to Alex, who was still to his right. Ewald had a large smile, and Alex looked like he would have started laughing any second, as if he was holding it in. After Ewald and Alex exchanged looks for about five more seconds, they both returned their attention to the tower. Julie held up a stick, one that looked nearly identical to the one Professor Katherine had held, the night before he came to Drolers. The only difference was the swirly design that was on the stick. She held it in the air, and the door slowly swung opened.

[22]

Chapter 5

The Golden Clock

The tower was empty, except for a set of spiral stairs at the back. Alex looked upwards and noticed that the stairs continued, going all around the perimeter of the tower, to the very top. "Okay, let's climb" Julie said not very loudly, as if she was tired. In fact almost everyone should be tired, as it was nearly an hour past midnight. "Do you know how to find the area of a circle?" Dhiman asked towards Ewald and Alex, but they didn't reply. Instead they just walked up against the curved black railing. As they walked up the white stone steps, everyone was talking to each other. Luckily, Dhiman hadn't asked another question for two minutes, which was probably the longest interval of time that he hadn't asked a dumb question in. Until he finally asked again, "If you multiply a positive number by a negative number, would the answer be positive of negative?" "That's it, could you please stop asking random questions, that nobody really cares about?" Alex nearly yelled because of how annoyed he was at Dhiman. They ascended up the stairs, and the whole way up Dhiman hadn't said anything.

The rest of the way up, everyone talked, but Dhiman said nothing. He was still a little surprised by what Alex had shouted previously. Every level higher Ewald would look out the windows that faced towards the fountain, the view got more, and more spectacular. Finally they had reached the top of the cylinder structure; there was another round room, like the one below.

[24]

A large gold clock sat on the nearly demolished column, which was in the center of the high room. A rug warmed the stone floor. The circular rug was a dark red and covered with blue and green writing; it looked as if it was the same language as the one Ewald had previously noticed on the fountain. The golden clock was engraved with roman numerals, all around the outside. It shined under the light that hung above it. Dhiman looked disappointed at the sight of the clock.

Behind the clock sat a portrait of a woman. She had long brown hair that stretched below her shoulders, and eyes that glittered like diamonds. She was wearing a light green robe, with a designed collar. Behind her stood a tall oak tree. The sky was unrealistically clear and blue. The woman had a kind smile on her face. A wooden frame surrounded the portrait, with a bronze plate on the bottom of the frame. The group stepped forwards to inspect the portrait. The bronze plate appeared to have the lady's name upon it; 'Aleena Estrand' said the plate. "Who is she?" Ewald asked Alex, but instead Dhiman answered. "She's one of the people who founded Tralbon" Dhiman blurted. Alex shook his head from side to side. "She died at the age of 62" Dhiman added. "When did her great-grandma die?" Alex asked sarcastically and humorously, "She actually died at the age 73, when she was working as an artist," Dhiman answered. "How do you know that?" Alex asked. "My mom gives me daily homework, I've packed nearly half my bag with papers," he said pointing towards the olive green bag he was carrying. Alex refocused his attention at the room.

A door to the right of the group stood leading into a long tunnel-like room. Julie walked up to the door, and the rest of the group followed. After, they were inside Ewald and Alex finally knew what it was, the view of a small lake below their very own feet, it was a bridge. A very long and narrow wooden bridge, it hung on for its life, from one side of the tower to another far away building. It wasn't based on ropes, it was made of solid wood, but it still seemed as if it would have ripped easily. Alex looked a little unsure about crossing this bridge, as it didn't have a very good base, and could break faster than a twig. The black lake sat silently in the darkness, not a single light was shining. Except for the high up moon, a third hidden by the clouds, that floated above them. They all walked together; because of the width of the bridge the maximum of people you could have beside each other was three. As you would have expected, Ewald, Alex, and Dhiman all walked together. Although Alex didn't seem too glad that Dhiman was there, Ewald wanted to give him a chance.

The group walked further, Ewald and Alex (same as everyone else) were looking out of the large windows, admiring the landscape. Far off mountains looked as if painted with oil pastels, and the lake painted by a soft and gentle brush. As usual, Dhiman looked as if the scenery bored him.

They were now three-quarters into the bridge. Dhiman leaned towards Ewald, "Do you think that this bridge could break, if a troll smashed his hammer into it?" Dhiman asked Ewald, quieter than he had asked before. It seemed as if Dhiman was trying to avoid contact with Alex, who had almost yelled at him before. "I'm not sure, I never met a troll" Ewald replied, "Oh," Dhiman said looking back out into the night. Right now, Alex was feeling kind of bad about yelling at Dhiman. "I'm sorry" Alex said facing Dhiman and Ewald, "For what?" Dhiman asked, although he knew what it was about. "You know, for yelling right at your face, which was very rude of me, and for interrupting you. I think I might have been overwhelmed by all the magic," Alex said. "Or, you could have just been jealous - of my smartness" Dhiman bragged. Alex was now even madder than before, and Ewald was surprised of Dhiman's response, to Alex's apology. Dhiman was just smiling at Alex's red face, Alex really wanted to punch him, but he couldn't. Well, he probably would have, except that now Ewald was trying to get Alex calmed down, by blocking Dhiman's face. In a few minutes, Alex was calm, Dhiman was still smiling, and they were at the end of the bridge.

An arched door, which looked as if made of old, scraps of metal, the kind you would find at a junkyard, sat in front of Julie. Everyone enter the empty room. It was just a hollow room, with nothing inside of it, except for the children who had just entered. The room extended high above their heads, but there were no stairs or ladders or any other way of getting to the top. As everyone was examining the circle room, Alex noticed that the door had disappeared silently. Alex tapped Ewald to show him that the door was missing, after he got Ewald's attention, he pointed at the spot where the door had been. Ewald understood quickly, and obviously since Dhiman had nothing else to do, but stand beside Ewald, he also noticed. Soon everyone knew, because Dhiman had nearly shouted out about the door. Now they were trapped.

All the kids were looking around the empty cylinder for a way to get out. Although Julie knew what was going to happen, she didn't say a word to any of the others. Some students even went around the wall, feeling and pushing the bricks, to find out if there was a hidden exit. Ewald and Alex were now looking around the room; they glanced at the room from bottom to top. Finally, they found something, a thick piece of metal running around the wall. The metal was as tall as a normal bedroom, and was hung from the top of the room. Alex's neck was a little tired, so he looked back down at the ground. Alex was sure that the piece of metal had not been there when he looked up at the ceiling when they had entered the room. "Maybe it was just camouflaged" Alex thought. Now, Alex refocused himself to the metal ring, the metal appeared to have moved down slightly. Alex pointed it out to Ewald, but this time Dhiman was looking at his old cell phone, so he didn't pay any attention to anything else. The piece of metal inched another foot towards them. This appeared as a problem.

Then, with one huge rush, everything happened. As everyone was staring up at the ceiling, the rusty metal ring flew towards them, carrying a big gust of wind after it. Everyone had a late reaction. People covering their faces, people pacing, people screaming, and some people were even diving towards the ground and curling up into a ball. There was a large boom from the impact of the metal on the brick stone, which nearly shook everyone there. The remains of the wind slowly disappeared and everyone's heart rate was beginning to slow down. The only one who didn't notice and experience what had just happened was the only person using their phone. Finally, he looked up at Ewald and saw that the wall in the background was now covered in metal. All the students began to look at each other. About twenty seconds later the ground began to rise, lifting with it the metal wall which now covered the old brick one.

The shock of the floor moving did make a few people jump, but it wasn't as horrifying as the metal wall falling. "Wow, I wonder how this works, It's awesome" Alex said amazed by the magic. "It's not that impressive really, it's kind of like an elevator. You know what those are, right?" Dhiman yelped at Alex. Alex's blood started to boil again, "Yes, I do, and you'd better shut your..." Alex stopped, he was trying to forget about it and calm down. His grandfather always told him that yelling and fighting would never get you anywhere in life, and in this case it was college. Dhiman crossed his arms; he put on a big smile, trying to get Alex even more outraged. It took the floor another fifteen seconds to get to the top, nearly half as fast as an elevator. Finally, it had stopped.

Chapter 6

Sorted

The metal then disappeared into a white smoke, and left. One part of the wall used to be covering an entrance to a hexagonal room. Everyone stepped out to the room. A glass ball the size of a square table glittered in the artificial light, which was pressed into the ceiling. After the ball sat three doors with almost nothing visible after. Everyone gathered around the glass ball.

On the shiny ball was a sentence, "Welcome to Tralbon." The writing was in a very large and clear font written in white, which matched the background of the ball pretty nicely. After, everyone had read it about another two or three times, a soft female voice repeated it in a loud whisper. Ewald looked around the hexagonal room for the voice, he expected there to be a women. He didn't find her. Then, the writing changed, "the oldest and finest magic school" it said, and the voice repeated. For the first time Alex found Dhiman excited, apparently Dhiman hadn't been to this part of Tralbon. The writing has once again changed, "I will always be here to help" and as usual the voice followed. "If you get lost, or if you're about to fail your exams" the voice paused in the middle of the sentence, and then continued. "By now you may be wondering about the three doors" because of the amount of words, the font had shrunk. Again the voice repeated. As the words faded out, three arrows appeared, each pointing to a door. Slowly words appeared below each arrow. The word in the middle said "West", and to its right "South" was written, on the other side "North" was under the arrow. "These doors lead to other parts of the school" it wrote and said. By now, Alex was beginning to think that the crystal ball was both writing and saying the words.

[32]

"Now if you may, please proceed to the north part of the school" the ball said and showed. Everyone walked to the right, and to the north part of the school.

It was at first dark, but a row of lanterns lit up with fire, sitting in the dark on both sides of the tunnel, waiting for someone to arrive. It really didn't look like a far distance to walk, but all the students were tired, so it seemed nearly doubled to them. After they got to the end, there was a locked door. The wooden door had a plank that looked as if made of gold; the plank had words dug into it. So everyone began to read on their own.

> "To the North you shall pass,
>
> If you get me what I ask.
>
> The answer to the following riddle,
>
> Please answer loudly like a fiddle.
>
> At night they come without being fetched.
>
> By day they are lost without being stolen.
>
> What are they?"

One-by-one they finished reading, and started to look at their acquaintances. After almost everybody was done, Julie finally said something, instead of letting the group find out things for themselves. "So, what do you think the answer could be?" Julie asked. "Well..." a tall boy called out, "The riddle says 'they come without being fetched' so they must have legs or something to move them" he answered looking at the gold plate. Everyone thought for a couple of seconds, "Well, does anyone else have a comment?" Julie asked. Dhiman put up his hand, which was a little awkward. Julie looked at Dhiman, "What if they didn't move they just get hidden or disappear" Dhiman said, moving his hands back and forth for no reason. "I would think that this riddle would be applicable to any region of Earth, so, it should be seen everywhere, not just in North America" Alex replied smartly, he thought he was starting to sound like Dhiman, which to him was not a good sign. "It could be the moon" Ewald said unsurely, "Actually no, it says it is more than one object" Dhiman howled at Ewald. Then a girl with long ginger hair from behind them seemed to have an answer, "I think the answer is the stars." "That's what I was going to say" Dhiman lied. Then, Julie turned to the door and said "Stars" in a loud and seemingly proud voice.

The door had opened, and the place was beautiful. Although it was different, it was still amazing. Unlike all the other rooms in the school, this one had a floor made of wood, like the dorm room Ewald and Alex had slept in the night before. The walls were made of the same old looking bricks, like the rest of the academy. On the far wall laid a poem.

"What side you shall be entered in, Is not based on what you want, But on your personality. These will act as teams for our soccer tournaments"

"What are you doing?" Ewald asked Dhiman, "I'm examining the pictures," he answered pointing to the left wall and then the right. He finally noticed the pictures, which he didn't know how he could not see them. The picture on the left wall was of a tall thin girl. Although she looked older, she still had a smile as innocent as a child's. Her light blue eyes glittered in the painting. Her black hair that stretched well below her shoulders was very noticeable against her pure white skin. The girl's nose was rounded, and her smile was soft and gentle. Then Ewald turned his head towards his right. Unlike the other picture this one was of a man, who looked in his young twenties (Although you couldn't see all of his face). The painting looked as if it was about the medieval times. The man had armor that covered every part of his body, the only hole in his knight costume, was a small rectangle that ran across his eyes. The silver armor looked like it could protect you from many weapons. In the knight's right hand he held a sword, pointing it upwards leaning to the right, in his other hand he held a shield; the shield was in the shape of a crest. An inch around the crest was a golden layer, with a silver layer inside. On the silver part of the shield sat a picture of a dragon. The dragon was of an orange color, and had a set of two large wings, that were bigger than the dragon was. A golden frame surrounded both paintings, but they had no background as if painted onto the wall.

Everyone had now seen the pictures and the writing. Just then, in the middle of the room appeared a stool, as if it had just faded in. On top of the stool sat a small squished cube, with a curved imprint of a hand. "Could everyone please make a line?" Julie said. Everyone made a line that reached even before the riddle door. Julie stood to the left of the stool. Ewald was second in line, with Alex after him. Dhiman was fifth in line. A boy stepped up to the box, and he placed his hand on the concave hand. To his surprise it fit him perfectly. About three seconds later, a small television-like object came out from the stool, to it's right. The screen was black, until it turned on by itself. In seconds it flashed through his life. On the screen he saw pictures of his house, friends, family, places he's been, thing his done. To the boy it was pretty scary. Then, a loud radio voice with a Scottish accent said "Katnor." The voice surprised some people and made some jump. When the boy finished, he turned around to face the rest he had a pleasant smile on. Then, he walked over to the painting of the girl, and stood in front of it waiting for everybody to finish. The boy nor Ewald and Alex knew why he had stepped towards the longhaired teenager; it was as if by force.

 Next up was Ewald, who was as nervous and scared as he could ever be. He took a step towards the stool and placed his right hand on the imprint. The black screen turned on, and it flipped through his life, as if it was a book. Images rushed at his eyes, one after the other. Soon, he began to see the oak tree, his family's house, his mother, and then unexpectedly

Alex showed up, with no sign of Dhiman. Both Ewald and Alex had noticed Alex's picture, and they both didn't know why. To Alex it was like being accused of something you've never done, except this was not all that bad. Alex actually prized Ewald for being able to hold his temper on Dhiman. After, the screen had scanned all the pictures, it turned blank again, and then it shouted, "Selvin." Then, without thinking of it, Ewald walked to the opposite side of the boy before him, passing Julie smiling to her awkwardly. He was on the knight's side.

Ewald was hoping that Alex would get picked to go to the knight's side, but Ewald knew Alex had no choice. Now, it was Alex's turn, he stepped up to the hand imprint, and placed his hand over it. The screen then turned on, and started looking at Alex's life. Just as Ewald had gotten Alex on the screen, Alex got Ewald. Ewald's picture was of him with a light smile, in a completely black area, same as the rest of the pictures. "Selvin!" shouted the stool. Alex walked towards Ewald, with a smile that looked like it would explode. Joy filled both Ewald and Alex, but Dhiman didn't know what to think of it as. Alex and Ewald started to whisper to each other quietly.

It was Dhiman's turn. The girl before him (the

one who answered the riddle) was chosen into 'Selvin' same as the two boys before her. Dhiman looked impatient, he's father had told him about this, and that it is very important. Dhiman took a slow step; Alex thought it was to add Drama. Then, Dhiman looked to his right and left, viewing the two sides. He put his hand onto the imprint, while closing his eyes tightly. He strained every muscle in his body. It wasn't as scary as Dhiman had thought, he relaxed his body. From the side he looked pretty ridiculous, but it was very important to him. Same as the others the screen zipped through his life. He stared at it, waiting for the answer. There was no sign of Ewald or Alex on the screen, Dhiman was nearly disappointed. The anticipation of the answer was clearly visible on his face. Then, finally the screen went dark again, "Katnor" the screen announced. A smile spread on Dhiman's face, and he walked over to his left.

Everyone had now had a chance at the stool, and had been sorted into the two sides. Then, Julie stood in front of the hand imprint. Ewald had forgotten that Julie was probably also around his age, and might also be attending Tralbon school. Then, she placed her hand onto the box. The screen reactivated, it flew through pictures, and moments. Memories blossomed in her head, remembering great things. "Katnor" the screen announced, just seconds after it had gone black. Julie looked perfectly happy with the result, but unlike the others Julie didn't go join her side. She just stayed standing before the stool. "Okay now that we all know what house we're all in, let's get some rest," Julie said. "All you need to do to get into your lounges is to slightly push on the paintings," she said looking from one group to the other. Then, Julie walked over to the painting of the dark-haired girl, and began to lightly push. So, did the other group. Slowly both paintings opened at the same time. Each group began to enter, lifting up their legs to avoid tripping over the half-foot high bricks.

***

The Selvin room was colorful, bright and vivid color was nearly on everything. You could feel the coziness in the air. Nearly opposite of all the students there was a dark arched door; you could see the beginning of a staircase at the bottom. The room was in a tower, Alex noticed by looking out the windows. The windows stood to the right and left of the arched door. Fancy curtains hung above the two large windows. The curtains were red, matching the room's theme. Alex felt very happy and energetic, which seemed impossible, as it was very late at night. The room just made him smile. For the first time in the school, the floor was made of a softer material. There was a soft but thick carpet, which had a simple pattern. Wavy stripes going up and down the floor, one strip was yellow and the next orange, the pattern kept repeating. Alex was tempted to feel the carpet. He bent down; it was fuzzier than anything he had ever felt. Ewald looked towards him, and then Alex quickly sprang back up. In the middle of the room was a table. It was brown and looked very antique. On one side of the table was an old armchair. It had two armrests on each side. It was a little different than all the other furniture. It was orange with yellow flowers painted across it. The flowers came in different sizes and positions, and were smartly scattered all over the seat. Some people seemed to not like it, mostly boys. Ewald and Alex loved it; they thought it gave the room more light. On the other side of the wooden table was a long and skinny couch. Its redness looked a little darker than an average red, but it suited the room nicely. Beside the left window stood a bookshelf, but it wasn't exactly filled with books. It was a short bookshelf, it only had about four shelves. The top two were packed with metals, trophies and awards that either the students won or the house all together. There were even some pictures between the awards. The bottom two had books, neatly organized. Most of the books were thick, and looked a bit warn out. The books unlike the room weren't at all colorful. Browns, blacks, and grey dominated the two lower shelves. Other ornaments were around the room but they were less important.

Unguided, all the students that were put into Selvin began walking towards the arched door. They made a much-unorganized pile, slowly pushing up the steps. The stairwell was grey and dreadful; it almost sucked all the happiness out of you, unlike the lounging area. They had only walked up about nine steps, there was a split, and the staircase turned to two, diverting from each other. The two staircases were curled. In between the two staircases there stood a thin pointed wall, separating the stairs. Attached to the wall were two signs, in the shape of thick arrows, pointing opposite of each other. The top one said "Girls" and the one underneath had the word "Boys" painted onto it, in a red handwritten font. Without even thinking about anything the boys and girls split, going into the correct stairwell.

After the boys had climbed their staircase, a huge bedroom came into view. The floor was covered in red laminated wood, which Ewald could slip on very easily. As more and more boys came up, Ewald and Alex walked up and around the room. It was circular; Alex began to think if the builders of this castle liked circles. The wall used the usual brick. One thing captured all the boys' attention; this room had dark brown wooden beds. The beds were lined up in a very organized manner. They were spread out, having their backs towards the wall and their feet pointing out to the middle of the room. Between every few beds there would be a small cabinet, which was in the shape of a square. On top of the cabinets were small rectangular windows, hung vertically. One boy felt very tired so he decided to rest on the bed. Some boys stared at him for a couple of seconds, and then lifted the covers and slipped underneath them. Slowly more boys were in beds, so both Alex and Ewald choose beds beside each other, and both slept. After the last boy sat on his bed, the lights dimmed themselves, and everyone fell fast asleep. Dreaming about what had happened that day.

Chapter 7
The Clumsy Teacher

That night Ewald dreamt of his mother, but it wasn't at all like the one he had in Drolers. This dream wasn't about her; it was about her ring, her shiny emerald ring. It was her second most prized

[44]

possession, after Ewald. Ewald knew that was a fact, because she wore it almost every day, and when she didn't she would hide it in her wrinkled silver purse. You might have thought that her smile was directed to Ewald, but she was admiring the ring, like an old childhood memory. The dream was starting to scare Ewald; luckily it didn't last long, as he opened his eyes. The moon was still high up in the sky, not yet gone. The room was grey, Ewald looked towards Alex. Who was sleeping silently, he was resting for tomorrow.

Ewald woke up, the sunshine leaking in from the window between his bed and Alex's. He noticed Alex's bed empty, and then he slowly sat up. He looked at all the other beds, they were all empty. There was only one boy still in the room other than Ewald, who was just about to go down the stairs. "Hey, where did everybody go?" Ewald asked the boy, the boy stopped and turned to Ewald. "They all went to the common room, the lounge" he answered Ewald, and then he continued towards the staircase. Ewald slowly slid one foot to the ground then the other. He was still tired from the day before. He used all of his might to stand up. Ewald never liked to get up early in the morning, but by the look of things it didn't seem that early. Ewald walked to the grey staircase, and walked downwards. The two stairs collided and transformed into one. Once again, he was in the peaceful common room, except it wasn't as peaceful as he had remembered. The room was crowded with the students, still wearing the same clothing as yesterdays.

Ewald stepped into the center of the round room, he was still half asleep. Quickly a hand pounced onto his back, "Boo!" "Ahh" he screamed of fear, he attracted the eyes of many boys and girls. Ewald grabbed the hand and turned around; he was slightly relived to see Alex's smiling face. "I scared you so much" he said with a chuckle as he looked at his red face. "Oh, what ever" he said to silence his friend. "Time for class" Alexander said as he pulled Ewald by the hand.

They walked over the soft rug, and out of the door. The room was empty, the stool that was there the night before had disappeared. "So, what's our first class?" Ewald asked, assuming he was in the same class as Alex. "Potions" Alex answered, looking at Ewald, who was focusing on the ground. "Potions?" Ewald asked himself quietly. "Its like chemistry, except the potions can do amazing things," Alex explained, as they walked down the small tunnel. For another minute or two they didn't say anything, until they had emerged into the hexagonal room. "The tall man in the common room, told us to ask the ball for help" Alex notified Ewald. Both of them walked close up to the crystal ball, although Ewald tried to stay away from it. "Um, hello. We just wanted to ask about the potions room" Alex asked nervously, he had never talked to a crystal ball before. It took a few seconds for the ball to answer. "Oh yes, the potions classroom" the glass said. The moment the crystal ball sung those words with its voice, Ewald felt at ease. "Let me answer in the form of a rhyme. To answer your quest, travel west." The voice answered. Ewald this time ran ahead of Alex. He entered the center doorway; it had the exact tunnel shape as the one that lead north. It even had the same lanterns, lighting the way. Ewald slowed down, Alex caught up. There was a long silence, only disturbed by their shoes on the ground. They had reached the end. The door opened. Ewald and Alex both thought there would have been a riddle guarding this door just like how the other one did. "I guess this one has no password" Alex reflected. Unlike the other room that stood after the North door, this one was tiny. It was a small cube, grey instead of the bright bricks. They both looked around the cube. Ewald noticed a large spider sitting on its web, waiting for an insect to catch, in a corner. An extremely thin stairwell stood. "Time to go down" Ewald said. Both Alex and Ewald ascended down the stairs.

Everything was black; neither of them could see anything. Alex was scared of the dark, just because he didn't know what was behind the blackness. Alex was also afraid that Ewald would sneak up from behind him, to get revenge. "Ah,

Welcome to potions class" a strong but choppy voice said. Ewald kept walking down the stairs, wondering where the voice had come from. Ewald looked down at an angle; he could almost see the end of the stairs. They both walked to the bottom, a room was in front of them, and the smell of jasmine flew up to their noses. A calm soothing smile spread on Alex's face, he always loved the smell of flowers. The room had the same grey, dreadful, and soggy appearance. Ewald could even see dark green slime drooling out between two bricks. The two boys walked three more steps into the room, now they had a view of the whole place. Alex wasn't too pleased; the place reminded him of a horror movie he had watched.

The room was set up in a very organized manner. The center was like a walkway, leading up to the front desk. Three rows and four columns of long tables sat on each side of the empty space. Each table looked filthier than the other, the dark brown surface covered in dust, some even had mildew. Alex's disguised grew towards the potions classroom as he looked around. "Please sit down," the same choppy voice said. Ewald tried to figure out who said that. A medium height teacher stood behind the front desk, looking out towards the class. He had a bald rounded head, with two elf-like ears coming out on both sides. His skin was floppy, and he had wrinkles on his large forehead. After they both noticed him, Alex and Ewald walked to two empty seats and sat down. To

Ewald's surprise the seats were more comfortable then they looked. Three more students came into the class; their expressions weren't any different. "So, welcome to Tralbon, I am Professor Hegnorf" the teacher said. Someone in the second row chuckled. Professor Hegnorf glanced at the area where it had come from. "This is you're first day, the other four grades will come tomorrow. Well, as you may have noticed, we mixed some Selvin and Katnor into one class. We think it is best, so not too many sport rivalries are born," he said with a smile. Alex searched for Dhiman within the class, but he couldn't find him. "You will spend three years here, becoming a great extraordinarily skilled or powerful person" the teacher paused for a few seconds. "Some might call you a warlock, wizard, witch, or sorcerer, but what ever you will be you will be great. You will learn to brew potions, cast charms, handle magic creatures, and learn about the history of our world" he took a minute to think.

"I guess we can start off by creating a very simple potion, called 'Upwards Flight'. Now, this potion can make a person levitate or as some would call it fly" he said searching his desk. "Now, if I can just find the three ingredients" he told the class. He looked through his drawer, pulling mostly papers out. A smile of relief grew upon his face. "Ah, here they are" he said, "Do any of you know what these ingredients are?" he asked as he tried to clear up the mess. Three objects sat silently, a brown rock-like object, a pink feather, and a vial of a blue substance. Dhiman raised his hand, and Alex rolled his eyes, he thought of all the times Dhiman was going to annoy him. "The three are lemonbite meat, a female griffin feather, and a vial of pixie spit," Dhiman said quickly with his back straight. "That is correct," he said, winking at Dhiman. Then Alex talked without permission, "Wait are we gonna have to drink the potion?" he asked with disgust. Professor Hegnorf had a frown on his face, "Well of course, that's how a potion works, you drink it," he answered. Ewald looked towards Alex and back to the front. "We first have to pour the pixie spit, into this silver cauldron," he said, grabbing the vial and watching the topaz blue spit splash. "Now, remember the first ingredient to most potions is water, it is the base" the Professor taught. He set the now empty bottle in its original place, and picked up the lemonbite meat. Alex had heard of how dangerous lemonbite can be, his parents told him to never come near to one. Luckily it was already dead. "After the spit, you use a hammer to squish the lemonbite meat, and then into the pot" he said while at the same hammering the meat. When he was done he picked it up to show the class, thick brown liquid was flopping down from it. Then, he dropped it slightly too high, some of the mixture jumped into the air, falling back into place. "And finally you add the griffin feather. You only dip it into the potion, you don't want to find a feather in your mouth" he said with a soft chuckle. The professor held the feather in his right hand, dabbing it slowly in and out of the potion. "And, now we turn on the heat for five minutes" he muttered, while reaching around to the front of the cauldron, and turning the heater which was underneath. He turned his wrist and pulled his hand back around. The teacher looked straight at the class; there was a long awkward silence.

"So, how do you like Tralbon?" Professor Hegnorf asked the students. He walked to his right, his hand sliding on his desk. A paper he forgot to put away got caught under it. He dragged it, not even noticing he had it underneath his hand. The students noticed. He continued walking and waiting for a reply. The paper slid beside the mini silver oven, and caught on fire. The old man still didn't see it, until the smoke rose, and surrounded him. The fire quickly burned through the paper and made its way to the wooden desk. The teacher gave out a squeal, as the students panicked. They all stood up almost in unison, together they began to run. The smoke grew even more, as they all fled the classroom. Alex was terrified of fire; he hadn't liked it since the day of the incident. He remembered his mother crying while the firefighters told them the outcome. He lost his older sister that day, and his mother had lost her daughter. Tears were brought to his eyes, at the thought of that day. Alex tried to hide his tears, but Ewald had seen them. Ewald at first believed that the smoke made him cry, Alex cried harder, and Ewald assumed otherwise. Everyone kept running up the stairs, through the tiny room, and out the south door. They all rushed through the tunnel, flooding into the hexagonal room. Their potions teacher ran behind them. The crystal ball suddenly flashed on, it released a loud bell. The students froze to the sound, but the teacher didn't. He ran around with his hands on his ears, he truly looked horrified. Finally, he looked around and stopped. Attention flew to him, as embarrassment filled his head. The professor then ran out of the room, and down to the elevator- like room. He waved goodbye as his class watched him vanish slowly, from bottom up. "Did he just leave?" Ewald pointed out with panic on his face.

Professor Hegnorf ran out of the room and onto the bridge. He looked out the open bridge, the sunlight shined over the lake. He took his hands out of his large brown pockets. He pointed at the lake with one hand, and slightly waved the other. Then, his hands turned to make a circular shape, as if he was holding an invisible ball. The center of the lake bubbled, as a lump of water jumped out, and froze in mid-air. With a quick gesture towards himself, the chair-sized ball of water ran behind him. He turned around and ran, still maintaining the sign. Until he emerged into the hexagonal room, all the students staring at him. Then, with a flip of his wrist, the wet ball went flying towards the west. It drove it self down the stairs and into the room. It sat for a minute then it exploded sending water everywhere. The fire died away, leaving a partially burned classroom. Ash was on the ground, and carbon dioxide slowly clearing away. Only his highly flammable bookshelf was alive, it was like a miracle.

Ewald had his jaw wide open, he was astonished, and everybody was. The very same man from the lounge came into the room, from the south passage. His long green robes sweeping the ground, as his 25 cm long beard waved from side to side. His large black eyes looked around the room; he glanced at the kids' worried faces. "What has happened here?" the man asked curiously. "Um, well, you see..." their teacher muttered. A tall ginger boy walked forward, "He saved us, and the classroom. It was set on fire" he stood up for his teacher. "Oh, I see. And what started the fire?" the man fought back. The boy stepped back he can't make their teacher sound innocent. The old man looked back at Professor Hegnorf. "Well, you see it was me, by accident" he admitted, even the students could see the fear on his face. The man looked towards the kids, and smiled. "Well, I am glad it didn't hurt anybody. Don't let it happen again," he said in a less strict voice as he left back to the south. The professor relaxed himself. "Wow, that was great magic" Alex told his teacher. The other students had the same thought. "Well, I don't only create potions, I also know both hand and wand spells" he said. "I don't know what to do now that we have a burnt classroom," he admitted. "I guess we can head outside, you know, get some fresh air" he said. All of the students loved his idea, especially now that the thick grey smoke had begun to rise from the west. "Okay, if you would follow me, I'll lead you out" he said to his coughing class. Then, he turned around towards the elevator room, sighed then began to walk.

They all levitated downwards, the air became cleaner. The wooden bridge sustained their weight, as they walked across it. Finally, at the end, they went into the 'East Tower'. The golden clock was still frozen at twelve sharp. They wandered past it and the painting, and down the stairs they ran. The stairs were beginning to bore a lot of people, starting with Dhiman. At last they could see the end, as they jumped at the sight. Professor Hegnorf in front leapt out side. The entrance wasn't at all like how it had been the night before, in fact it was brighter, and it made you feel happier. Although the fog still remained you could see almost every part of the place. The professor signaled them to his left. A hole the size of a door was carved into the hedge wall. Everyone followed the professor, and walked into the hole.

They all emerged from it and into a pasture. An open field of grass sat under the light sun. The fresh air was moving around them. There was no breeze in the beginning, but the wind picked up, blowing towards them. To their left was a room-sized lake engraved into the earth. A forest waited behind it, the forest was wide and vast, but it wasn't filled with trees. The empty green forest was silent, except for a couple of chirping birds in the background. The old bridge could be seen to their top left, still holding onto the sides of the two buildings. With a quick twist their teacher was directed to them. "Go ahead have fun, just don't wander into the forest, or fall into the lake. You have no idea of how many people have fallen into it," he ordered nicely. Ewald thought about what he had just said, and then walked away in the direction of the open space. Alex followed Ewald a little faster. As usual Dhiman also walked towards the hexagonal room. Nobody said anything; the three would occasionally glance at each other. "I don't think that many people could have fallen into that lake" Dhiman said, "He probably said it to scare us" he pointed out. "Or maybe tons of people have fallen in" Alex said loudly in an angry voice. Dhiman retreated; sometimes Dhiman thought Alex had problems in his life, just because he was always forceful. Ewald looked around, "Yeah, and I don't see why we can't go into the forest, it looks perfectly fine" Ewald added. "Once I heard there is a spell guarding it and whoever enters will regret it," Dhiman whispered in a mysterious voice. "You really believe that stuff?" Alex asked, "Well, of course" he answered. Everyone paused.

 Two girls came up to them. Both of the girls had long hair, and were fairly tall. One girl had shiny brown hair, her almond eyes looking at the boys. The second one of the two had dirty blond hair, a wide smile, and glittering blue eyes. "Hi" both of them said together, they looked at each other. "Hello, I'm Sophie" the brown haired girl said, pushing the other girl out of the way. "And, I'm Violet" she told the boys. Alex silently raised his hand to welcome them, while Dhiman tried to ignore the two. "Um hello I'm, I'm, I'm" Alex muttered, "His name is Alex, and I am Ewald" he spoke for him. "So, what are you talking about?" Sophie asked. "We were talking about the chances of falling into that lake" Dhiman answered, pointing at the large pond. Neither the boys nor the girls knew what to talk about; Ewald just hoped his school year wouldn't be just silence. "Do you want to...? Um" Violet said, "Want to play..." Sophie paused to think, "Hide and Seek," she blurted out. "Sure" Ewald said without thinking about it. The other boys stared at Ewald, as if asking him to take it back. "I'll count" Violet said, and then she closed her eyes and began from one. "One, Two..." Ewald ran towards his Professor, and hid behind him. "Three, Four, and Five..." Alex looked at the forest and noticed an ancient ruin. He jogged to the side of the forest, and stood behind the stone archway. "Six, Seven..." Sophie panicked, scanning the area. With a few seconds she was blending in with the rest of the class, trying to hide her face. "Eight, Nine..." The remaining hider sprinted towards the dark green hedge, heading into the cut out whole. Even though Dhiman knew not to exit the boundaries, he disregarded them. "Ten, ready or not here I come" Violet yelped, she opened her eyes, and began to look. Her long hair whipped as she spun in all directions. Just as she began to walk in the opposite direction of Sophie, she heard a loud deep voice. "Hey, why are you here?" a boy asked, and then Sophie appeared out of the group. Sophie slowly backed off, trying not to show him her fear. Then, with a bend of his elbow, she flew backwards and into the lake. She dived, the teacher quickly ran exposing Ewald. The other boys ran towards the lake. Sophie jumped, bobbing for air, her hair covering her eyes. She panted. Professor Hegnorf pulled open his pocket, and pulled out a very similar stick. He aimed at the last spot he had seen Sophie, and strained his body. She shot up into the air a couple meters, and plopped to the ground. Water gurgled in her open mouth, her body shivering. The professor leaned closer to her, no one dared to talk. Sophie grasped for a breath, as she nervously opened her eyes. "Oh, thank god you're okay" the professor said meaningfully. She pushed her hands down on the soggy ground, leaning forward. Her face frightened, as her heart pumped as if she had just ran a kilometer. Sophie looked at the boy who had pushed her and frowned. "Come on" he said as he flung Sophie's arm around him, "Let's get you inside." The teacher began to walk in the opposite direction, as they had come from. The rest of the class lagged behind.

Chapter 8

An Old Secret

Ewald wondered about the huge buildings that stood to his left, they looked so much grander than they felt from the inside. He thought about the rest of the mansion, as he walked gazing to his left. "Soon, we'll be inside the school, and you can all eat' the professor howled directing it mostly at Sophie. She walked shivering; as a breeze would fly by her teeth would jump. The round boy who had pushed her, walked behind everyone. Every once in a while people would look back at him, with a questionable stare. It took the class a journey, as they turned around the school walls, and finally came to a stop. A glass walled room sat, attached to the school. Dhiman had seen many buildings but he had never seen a room with this shape. The transparent room was in the shape of a half circle. As usual the class got into the room, and as the invisible door closed the room began to rise. The class was amazed at the exceptional view, the endless forest all around them. Then, the light bricks on the school vanished, and the class walked out of the opposite side. "So, that was an elevator?" Alex asked. "Oh yes, but it was quieter. Which is why it's so magical" the teacher answered. "Really" Alex muttered to himself. The thought about calling an elevator magical just because it created less noise seemed dumb to both Alex and Ewald. The class walked past the doors of the two lounges, and through the north tunnel.

Finally, they had reached the hexagonal room. It seemed as if they were walking in circles around the school. Everyone proceeded towards the west, following their teacher. The smoke had by now somewhat cleared out, and they all could breath perfectly. Then, the teacher turned and led the way west. Sophie could see the grey cube room. "Okay, we need to go group at a time" Professor Hegnorf called. So, the class split up into multiple groups. The professor, Sophie, and about five other students got into the room first. While the others stood behind the open door. Just as the other room flew up, this one was also a hidden elevator. The floor under Sophie's feet suddenly dropped, at first it was fast but it eventually slowed down. If the students had noticed (which a few did), then they would have known that only the floor was moving down, as the ceiling or walls did not move. The professor and students got off and entered another room. Expeditiously the floor shot back up, and the next group of students flew down. After all the other groups had gone, it was Ewald's group's turn. Alex, Ewald, the boy who pushed Sophie, and two other girls, climbed into the room. Quickly they dropped.

This room was lighter. High up lights glittered, as the slippery walls reflected the brightness. None of the students could see anything, until their eyes adjusted to the light. The room was vast; it extended outwards then turned left. Small square table were organized, with eight chairs surrounding them. All five students walked out, and the floor pounced into position. Nobody was there except for Ewald's class. "Okay now, you will be having three meals in here. There will soon will be a very convenient food picker but for now, go grab your food from over there." Professor Hegnorf said, as he turned around and walked with Sophie.

Sophie and the professor walked to the back of the enormous room. "So, tell me Sophie. Do you know that boy who pushed you?" he asked looking straight at his student. Sophie kept her head pointed to the ground, "Uh yes, I know him. He was in my old neighborhood," she said shyly. "Oh, and you know him how?" the teacher investigated. Sophie didn't answer, "Is everything okay?" he asked. "Um, yeah" she said, raising her hand to her cheek and wiping her tears off. "Are you sure there is no problem with me asking this?" he asked out of politeness. "Yeah sure, it's just that, we didn't get along very well" her voice low, and weak. "Is there something I should know about? You know to look out for," he said. They both stopped walking, Sophie turned to Mr. Hegnorf. "I think I'll be fine" she reassured, "Now, I'll go talk to Robert" he mumbled just loud enough for Sophie to hear. He turned around and walked to him, and Sophie did the same.

Sophie stopped on her way to Ewald, dried her

tears, and tried to look happy. "Are you okay?" Ewald asked sympathetically, she nodded her head. All three boys could see behind her fake smile. "Who is he?" Dhiman asked, without thinking of Sophie's feelings. She stared at him, he quickly backed away understanding. "He's Robert Pulinski, he used to live in my old neighborhood," she answered. "Is there something wrong?" Alex asked, "No. Uh, how about we go get some breakfast," she suggested. All four students walked to the carts filled with trays of food, they had the exact same food as the hospital did. They all went and sat at a square table in the middle of the room, and began to eat. "Are you gonna eat that?" Alex asked pointing at Ewald's plate, "No, you can have it" he replied. Quickly Alex grabbed the plate and began eating it first, just in case Ewald asked for it back. "Why aren't you eating" Sophie questioned concerned, "I just don't feel hungry" he lied, "And I really don't like dragon eggs that much." Sophie turned her head to Dhiman then back at her food. "Hey, where's Violet?" Sophie asked quietly, "Not sure" Ewald responded to her question.

"Sophie" a voice yelled down the room, the professor walked with the chubby boy. "I think Robert has something to say to you," he said looking at the boy. Robert glanced at the ground then back up, "Umm, I'm sorry for pushing you," he said in the laziest and most inconsiderate voice in the world. "And" the professor added, "And I promise I won't hurt your feelings anymore." "Thanks" Sophie said not knowing what else to say. "Well, I guess my work here is done, maybe I should sign up to be next year's guidance consular" Professor Hegnorf suggested to himself. In a couple of second they were both out of sight. After all the students had finished breakfast, they headed up stairs for their next class. Within minutes they quickly were vanishing up the cube.

Chapter 9
Halloween Hunt

Weeks passed, everything was fine. Even Alex was beginning to become less annoyed of Dhiman's non-stop talking. Ewald and Alex worked hard in class, creating potions, learning spells, and handling magical creatures. Almost everything in Tralbon School was great. All the other students from the other four years got settled in, and were beginning to work. Time had passed by like a day, but it was nearing the end of October. The school watched as the forest turned from green to light orange, the air becoming colder. It was almost nine thirty, that's when the 'Halloween Hunt' would begin. All the students got the chance to go to the nearest town 'Slungon', and buy Halloween costumes. The whole school was excited.

Ewald stood in front of the Selvin door; he was wearing a Dracula costume. His long cape was reaching the ground. Ewald's face was painted white, fake fangs hung from his mouth, red paint drooling down to his chin. Ewald stood there waiting for Alex to come out with his costume on. He wanted it to be a surprise. The door opened and out came Alex. He was wearing a long red cape, and a golden crown. "It's not the best costume, but it will do" Alex said looking at his own costume. They both walked down to the crystal ball room, and into the South pathway. Dhiman ran up from behind Ewald, it reminded them both of their meeting. Dhiman was slightly sweating, which really wasn't at all noticeable under his curly white wig. Dhiman wore a long lab coat. "Can you guess who I am?" Dhiman asked both of them. "Thomas Edison or some other dead guy" Alex answered. "No, I'm Albert Einstein" Dhiman said, frowning at Alex. Ewald seemed impressed with the costume. "So, what are you?" he asked forcefully towards Alex. Alex rolled his eyes, and ignored his question. Instead Ewald took the question, "I'm Dracula," he answered with a smile. Ewald always hated when people fight, and recently Dhiman and Alex have been at each other throats. Ewald tried to keep smiling, while trying to separate the two. Then, they resumed walking in the slight darkness. They reached the end of the passage, the same door also stood. It was decorated in cheap Halloween ornaments; a glow in the dark skeleton, large jack-o-lantern signs, bones, and other decorations. None of the three were impressed.

    Alex pushed the door open, a trapezoid shaped room pointed at them. Two tunnel ways cut into the wall in front, with two doors to their left and right. None of them could see past all the decorations, and the woman who was handing out flyers. "Why hello" welcomed the tall dark blonde teacher, "This is what you need to do" she said giving each of them a ticket. At the same time they all glanced at their papers.

'This is Tralbon's 87th annual Halloween Hunt. The Halloween hunt is an opportunity to take a break from work, and have fun. The south section of the school has been shut down for this event. During this event students will, run around

looking for candy. Hidden behind traps, that will need the students to use the knowledge they have learned, and to enforce it in everyday life. You may begin'

Alex looked at Ewald and shrugged. Together the boys ran through the tunnel on the left and made a left turn. They quickly jogged to the history classroom. "So where is the candy?" Dhiman asked, "We need to look for it, we don't know" Alex yelped. "It was a rhetorical question" Dhiman replied, as he shook his head. They split up and begun to search. Ewald treaded over to a small wooden cabinet, while Dhiman searched the teacher's desk. "Hey, I don't think we're allowed looking through his things" he pointed out to Dhiman. "Maybe it's in here, how would you know?" he replied, trying to argue his case. Alex just stood at the door thinking, "Did you find anything?" he asked Dhiman. "Nothing but junk" he answered offensively, Ewald wasn't too happy of his statement. "Oh, I think I know where the candy is" Alex said excitedly. "Do you remember those movies where there is always something hidden behind or in a bookcase? Well, let's check there" he suggested. The other two boys hopped of the floor and ran to the bookshelf. "Check behind the books" Ewald bellowed. The three students shoved the books back and forth, "Do you see any candy?" Dhiman asked. "No" Alex answered, and then with a huge blast a small opening between two dictionaries shot out candy. The tiny sweets flew to the end of the room, and the boys ran after them. "Wait how did we use magic?" Alex noticed. "Yeah, that wasn't hard" Ewald said agreeing with his best friend. In a few seconds ten students jerked into the classroom. "What do we do, they're gonna steal our candy?" Ewald panicked; "They're not real, but they will take them" Dhiman informed the others. Within a couple of moments, the trio was blasting the dummies with their hand magic. Ewald gestured a push in the air, and the students flew to the wall. Dhiman did the same. Alex tried to push the dummy, then with a whip, a students wacked him across the face. Alexander fell to the ground; Dhiman pointed at him and pulled his own arm upwards. He jumped off of the floor, and began to fight. With a flick of a finger, the final doll fell smack on its face. "We'll just take that," Alex said grabbing a piece of candy from a student's hand. The three went around picking of every last sweet on the ground. "Okay, let's go to the next room" Dhiman said, carrying the candy in the folds of his arms.

They walked back out through the passageway. "Oh, I'm glad to see you again" the tall thin teacher said. "I forgot to give you your candy bags," she said handing them each a plain dark orange bag. "Well, bye" Alex said, just as they were about to leave into the right tunnel. They made a quick right, behind that there was another intersection. "Which way do we go?" Dhiman asked, "Let's go left, again" Ewald proposed. He led them for another 15 meters, and then another door waited. A gigantic cube room stood, it seemed as if it was the school's library. To all three of them it was enormous. Dark wooden shelves stacked up to the ceiling, packed with thick books. There even was a movable ladder, and an external floor attached as a second floor. "Wow" Alex exclaimed, "I know right, this is huge" Ewald cheered. "Way bigger than my old school's, and come on Pertons Academy is big" Dhiman confessed. Alex walked into the room, "Let's find the candy," he echoed. Unlike the history room this one was already filled with people. "Are they dummies?" Ewald asked, "Do you want me to give them an IQ test?" he answered thinking his joke was funny. Ewald stared at him, "Fine don't laugh, and no they are not fakes," he finally answered. Alex looked around the room, "So, you're saying we need to find candy in this huge room, filled with other people also looking for the same candy?" Alex asked concerned. "Yep" Ewald verified. "Maybe, there are more than one stash of candy in each room, for the next group" Dhiman smartly added. "Where do you want to look first?" Dhiman asked directed at his more favored classmate. "It's probably not inside the bookcases" he answered, "Maybe it's on the second floor" he replied. Alex just paused, looking back and forth between the two others.

This time Dhiman led the group up the light

wood stairs, which looked cheaper than ever. They arrived to the second platform that sat above seven meters from the carpet-covered ground. A lengthy rectangular table sheltering the rugs below had a few pupils reading around it. "Wait, the whole school is doing the Halloween hunt, right" Alex asked, "Yeah" Ewald answered his new friend. "Then, why are they looking through the books? You don't think that they think the candy is in there?" he replied, "Alex is right" Dhiman muttered trying not to be noticed crediting him. "But, what if they're wrong?" Ewald said, "Well, we'll just have to take the chance" Dhiman replied, walking over to the bookshelves. "Let's try this one," he said pulling a thick worn out brown book. It was jammed between the two other books. Dhiman pushing his fingers tightly around the outsides of the book. He relived as his fingers slid through, then he clutched it and pulled.

    He leaned back putting all of his weight into it, as Alex knew Dhiman was the weakest 11 year-old he had ever seen. He kept on tugging even thought he knew he should give up. With a jerk the book flew of the shelf, Dhiman flew back with it. He trampled over his feet, hitting a ginger haired girl named Suzy in the back with his sharp elbow. Suzy nearly fell down to the ground below, if the railing around the platform hadn't saved her. The three books that were in Suzy's arms jumped, and nearly hit other students. Suzy froze of shock, staring at Dhiman. "What have you done? You could have pushed me over the edge" she screamed, "And, that's not all. You also could have killed that kid down there. So, next time you want to injure people, don't do it near me" she finished as she walked down the stairs to retrieve her books. Dhiman blushed of embarrassment, and stood silently staring at where the girl had been. Alex snickered, not at the fact that he almost killed two people, but at Dhiman's face.

"Come on, lets look" he encouraged, trying to open the book. "Hey, what's the name of that book?" Ewald questioned, "It's called 'History of Halloween'" Dhiman answered flipping the book over. "Could you please pass that one to me?" he asked Alex. He pulled the one to its left off the shelf, "This one's called 'Halloween Secrets'" he answered without being asked. "And, can you open it?" he asked back, "No" he answered struggling with the book. Ewald's face grew a smile, "So, that means the candy is in the Halloween books." "But they're locked" Dhiman said, repeating Alex's thought. "Now, we use magic" Ewald said, "We need to unlock it, so we need out wands" he pointed out to them. "Right" Dhiman congratulated, "Only wands can open and unlock items or doors." "Wow, you're so smart" Alexander shot back sarcastically.

The three pulled their magic sticks out of their pockets. "Okay just point your wands, and think about it being unlocked" Dhiman said, "We know what to do" Alex spoke out for the both of them. They closed their eyes to concentrate, and they thought. With a boom the thick books exploded with candy. The tiny sweets flew into the air like a furious fountain, and landed right back onto the books. "At least none of the students can get them," Alex whispered, although the whole library was staring at them. They pushed the candy into their bags evenly, and walked out. Yet again, they walked back out through the tunnel, and made a right turn. "Wait, I never came this way," Ewald noticed. Both Alex and Dhiman have never been here. "I wonder what room it'll be" Dhiman added annoyingly.

A darker room came into focus; the same bricks that were used in the potions classroom were also used here. "Ugh, what happened here? Did they run out of the light bricks?" Dhiman moaned, as Alex made a face at him. There was only one other male in the room. Robert looked at Ewald with anger, and then approached. "Hey, listen you better keep away from Sophie" he said in an urban accent, "What?" Alex protected Ewald. The large boy glanced at Alex with a fierce eye, and treaded away. "What was that about?" Dhiman asked Ewald, "Not sure" he replied slowly. "And we shall never know" Dhiman said circling his hands. Then, he looked around the cramped room. Cages stacked all around the outside of the classroom. Although the cages were too dark to see what was inside Dhiman had a guess. "Oh this is the magical creature's room, that's why there are cages everywhere," he said. "Where's the candy?" Alex asked as if that was the only thing he was thinking about at that moment. "Do you think it could be inside one of the cages?" Ewald asked Dhiman, "No, it would be too dangerous. What if they opened the wrong cage and a wild animal attacked the kid. The school would get sued" he replied. "Hey, there's a door over there" Alex pointed out, "Yeah, but that one leads outside" Dhiman said. "How would you know that?" Ewald asked suspiciously, "I have a map" Dhiman said with a thick smile. For some reason the two others didn't believe him. "But, we still don't know where to find the candy" Alex muttered. Dhiman didn't seem to care anymore as he pulled out a piece of candy and began to chew on it. Ewald looked around; he was so desperate that he even considered looking into one of the cages. Alex stared at the ceiling, "Is that what I think it is?" he asked just to get their attention. They all looked up, "Do you see it?" he asked pointing at the spot. "It looks like a small engraved box," Dhiman said. "Maybe the candy is in there" Ewald yelped excitedly.

"We need to open something, so we use our wands" Alex thought aloud. Once again the three pulled their wands out. They all cast the spell, while pointing their wands upward. With a gush, candy rained from the ceiling. The boys' faces lightened by the candy, then Alex frowned. "Again, we need to use magic" he said, "We just did" Dhiman replied in a nasty voice. "Oh, forgot" he reclaimed. They separated the pile of suckers, chips, gum, and other sweets evenly, and dumped it into their nearly full bags. They picked them up and left like nothing had happened. The boys ended up back at the trapezoid-shaped room. "Excuse me, where do we go when we're done?" Dhiman asked the tall blonde professor. "Oh, you go back to your sleeping areas, have some candy, and then go to sleep" she informed them in a sweet and gentle voice. "Thanks" Alex said for Dhiman, as he doesn't usually thank anyone.

  The two Selvin boys climbed into their beds, holding their flooded bags and dumping them on the beds. The room was dark and partly loud as the other Selvins talked about the day while eating their bag of candy. They gazed at their piles, "Wow, this is way more than I got at my old town" Alex said. "What did you get?" he asked Ewald, "Mostly mini chocolates, but some chips as well" he answered poking his heap of sugar. "Same here" he replied, "What's your favorite?" Ewald asked just to start a new conversation. "I like gum" he said chewing loudly, "Mm, strawberry" Alex added. "Let's eat some more and finish it tomorrow" Ewald suggested, packing up his candy back into the large recyclable bag. Just as they had done all the previous nights, they quickly sleep under the full moon.

Chapter 10

Losing a Dragon

It was into the beginning of the first week of November. The class had just finished breakfast, and was heading to their very first creatures class.

"I can't wait to learn about all the creatures," Alex said to Ewald who nervously walked beside him.

"I'm not sure about this. There's a reason we need a class for this, it's not like it's going to be about how to care for kittens" he replied with a speedy tone. The rest of the class seemed excited to hang around large dangerous animals that don't live outside of the magic section. "Well, if they expect me to go near one of them, they better be in a cage" he announced to the small group that walked nearby. The students neared the grey-bricked room. "And the professor better be understanding" he added, for the first time Alex wanted to roll his eyes at Ewald's complaining. "Don't worry; I heard it was going to be about violet pixies. I have two at home they're the harmless kind" he calmed him. The entrance to the cage room brightened, and a woman stood.

  The young professor's slim body matched her small head. Beady blue eyes hung above a large smile. Her head wore a straw sunhat with two green feathers on the back. "Is she one of the three musketeers?" Alex jokingly whispered, "And look at those adventurer boots, hope we're not heading for the jungle" he added. "Excuse me," she said for the class to hear, "What did you say?" she asked although she obviously knew the answer. She then directed her small eyes to the other students, "Welcome everybody to creatures class. As you may have heard today we'll be studying pixies, but I have changed my mind, and we will be beginning with something that may look more dangerous but really isn't" she stopped to look at their expressions. "Today, we will learn about baby dragons" she said, Ewald's stomach turned over. She saw most students looked scared, "Now they don't do anything. They haven't learned to fire breath, their teeth haven't grown yet, and even their claws aren't sharp. It's nothing really," she sourly admitted. The professor stopped to think for a minute, "Oh yes forgot, my name is Madame Selvia. Okay let's head outside" she suggested. The class followed like robots, through an arched door and down a half spiral staircase. They were back outside.

The green grass was dancing in the fall wind, the rain that fell the night before now in puddles. The students lumped together staring at the only object they hadn't seen while they were at Tralbon. A small classroom sized object was on the ground; it had a faded blue color and was only two inches thick. "Okay, so this is a short transporter. All of you should have been transported to Drolers, so hopefully you don't faint. Usually you only faint the first time" she informed them. After being transported to the hospital, Ewald, Alex, nor Dhiman felt nauseous about doing it again. "Now, when I step onto it you all have five seconds to get on" she said looking at the transporter. Professor Selvia stepped onto it; the class ran onto it almost pushing off the teacher. With a blue flash their eyes shut, and then opened.

Amazingly no one had fainted and even more

amazingly they all made it safely. To Alex's left he could see the very same lake that Sophie got pushed into, in fact none of the boys had talked to her since. Ewald looked down, there appeared to be a different transporter. A small fenced area to their right, which sat right at the edge of the forest. The white fence was in a rectangular position, with a small-extended section with a door like gate at the end. "Everyone walk off," she ordered angrily, "I forgot the cages," she muttered. They all walked off the transporter, and again she disappeared. Five minutes later she reappeared, but now she had dozens of cages. "Hurry up, everyone grab one fast, but don't touch the transporter" she advised. Ewald and Alex rushed to the side and grabbed a cage each. Ewald didn't dare look inside it, but Alex was already poking it with his finger. "Ah, how cute is he" he said to encourage Ewald. "Everyone when you are done getting a cage, come join me here" the teacher said pointing at the closed yard. After everyone got into the enclosed area, they automatically made a wall around the fence. Their professor seemed impressed. "Carefully set the cages on the ground" she instructed. The class did just as they were told. "Now here are some rules, only open the cage if I say so. And don't do anything that can harm the animals" she clarified with the class. "These baby dragons are from beyond the 'Hill of Hope' in our forest. Right now, they are more harmless than the Notty pixies," she said with a giggle, and then it grew into a loud wet laugh. "She calmed herself down, "What you don't get it?" she asked. "Today's youth aren't like I remembered," she said to the class in a gross manner.

"Okay so as I was saying, they are very harmless at this age" she repeated, smiling from reminding herself of the cheap joke. "Today we'll learn about the dragon, and the next time you have class here we'll review what you have learned," she told her excited class. "First, we'll talk about their diets" she said pulling out a dark green bucket, "Who can guess, what this bucket has?" she asked in improper English. None of the young adults raised their hand, not even Dhiman who sat across from Ewald. "Oh, nobody knows well that's okay. That is why we teach you this stuff" she said to make the students feel less unknowing. She looked around once more to make sure no one had the answer, "Okay I'll tell you, inside this bucket is skunk meat" she said in a calm voice. "Actually, you can use any type of meat, but they like the skunky flavor" she added to their knowledge. Alex looked back at his red and brown scaled dragon. "But, as I told you they don't yet have teeth. So, I already grinded them" she ruined Ewald's day. He felt like vomiting especially after breakfast, he kept thinking about the fact that they ate grinded skunk meat.

"As some of you may know, I like to have

some hands- on activities. So, I want you to pass the gloves around, then the bucket. Then, put the meat inside its cage through the bars. If you can't fit you hand, then open the door only slightly and keep watching it at all times" she sped through the instructions and handed the short girl beside her a bucket of gloves and one of smelly skunk meat. The students passed them around, first pulling on a glove then taking a handful of meat. Alex tried shoving his hand into the side, "Ugh, its not fitting. I don't want to open the door," he moaned just loud enough for his friend to hear. Ewald had his hand fit perfectly through, and began dropping the food on the cage floor. Alex opened the door just enough for his hand to leak into it. "Okay everyone, I'm going to pass the bucket around for a second time. It seems as though these scaled dragons are hungry," she announced.

Alex for just a second left sight of the cage door, as he turned around to pick up extra meat for the baby dragon. The dragon pushed the door with the side of its body, attempting to get more food. "Alex the cage's door is open," their female teacher shouted across to him, he looked back panicking, knocking the cage over. The teacher slightly relaxed as the dragon barely escaped from the falling cage. It opened its bumpy wings and hopped, then in a shot it flew up in the direction of the forest. It soared above Dhiman's head, before fading into the light trees, which have already started shedding their leaves.

Professor Selvia marched madly over to Alex. "Not only have you knocked over the skunk meat, you've also managed to let go of my favorite dragon" she muzzled with a loud snort. "We'll all miss him" she sadly lied, as the woman looked into the forest. Alex worried if this was going to affect his mark, and he also partly missed the cute creature. "Okay time to move on" she said, raising her hand to her forehead as a salute to the dragon. Ewald now knew the school's drama queen, and hoped she wouldn't volunteer as the new club manager. "Who knows where most dragons live?" she asked snapping herself into reality. Dhiman raised his hand waiting to happily answer. "Oh, how 'bout you?" the teacher said as she pointed at him, but before he had a chance to answer, it begun to rain. Large chunks of dirty water dropped overhead, and splattered into the grass. "Everyone onto the transporter" she yelped to them, and they all jumped onto it with their dragon cages.

They jumped off of the first transporter and ran up the stairs, crowded and pushing to get inside. Professor Selvia ran up the steps and tripped, falling straight onto her face. All of the students stopped, and started accusing each other of tripping her. "No, it wasn't anyone" she claimed pushing herself back on her feet. "Let's just continue in here," she said to them, making some of them unhappy. They all sat around in a pile with the cages. "Okay, so as I was saying, who knows where" she said before she was interrupted by a ruckus, that sounded like clanking pans falling. She turned; "behave yourselves, and take care of your dragons" she instructed them and left.

The petit teacher ran awkwardly trying not to fall again; as she grew closer to the main south room the sounds began to get clearer. She entered the trapezoidal room, and saw two other professors also there. "What was that sound?" she asked in a polite and professional voice. "He's looking for it" the taller of the two answered her. She frowned.

"And, wasn't it funny when she tripped over her own feet?" Alex joked without care to her feelings. "Well, not really" his best friend answer to him, he sat back. Ewald wondered about the sounds that they had been hearing for most of the day, "Hey, what do you think those loud sounds were?" he asked waiting for a mysterious reply from Alex. "Maybe the kitchen had a few problems" he suggested, "No, we wouldn't be able to hear it from here" he realized, he shook his head. "Well, there better not be a mash potato burglar" he tried to joke again, and both of the boys were laughing. "Wait, where is Dhiman?" Ewald noticed, they all looked around the cramped room.

"He was here a minute ago," he added.

Professor Selvia jogged back into her classroom, scaring everyone. "I need you all to head to the eating area, I know you were just there, but this is an emergency," she shouted, and in seconds they all were running out.

Chapter 11
The Missing Army

The first year class joined the rest of the school in the eating area. They all huddled onto a round table in the far left corner. Ewald and Alex sat beside each other, with Violet across from them. "I still don't see him," Ewald said referring to Dhiman. "Who,

Dhiman?" she asked, without waiting for an answer she added. "He told me he had to go somewhere urgent," she told the table. No one said anything, "How are we going to pass the time, this is killing me" she moaned while flipping her hair. "Oh, I know. We can tell stories" she jumped at the idea, just so no one else says anything more interesting. Alex rolled is eyes at the idea of telling stupid stories to people you barely know. "Here" she said thinking of one to say, "I'll tell you about a true story, which changed the magic section's history forever." She shuffled her chair around, as she thought of how to start. "Once there was a man, an evil man. He was lonely and felt powerless. He had a terrible childhood, and he grew more and more jealous of others. One day he gathered a group of people with the same intentions, and they joined together to fight against the magic government. They would break into shops, kill poor animals, and even kidnap other people" she stopped, to watch their expressions. "His army grew more and more powerful everyday, and at one point they were at a stronger position that the government. Not a single candle lit in their presence, no one talked, and no one played. It was like the ice age, but with crimes. Then, two powerful warlocks and a great witch came out to protect the magic section," Violet continued. Alex looked at Ewald as if he had just seen a black hole. She drank from her bottle then presumed, "The three were highly powerful, and mighty. One day, they faced him and his full army. It was three against over one thousand. The three used all of their power to save us from extinction. Sadly, they couldn't survive. After using all of their power, they were forced to become gems. The three of them turned to a different gemstone each, as a sign of their greatness. Their power could only vanquish his arm. The army disappeared but a single seed was left of them. It fell into the ground, and formed an oak tree, which is now hundreds of years old" she stopped for a break. "And it is said to be a very strong oak tree. It attracts any magic folk, almost like a love spell," she added. Ewald thought about it, for some reason he didn't really care about any other tree, only which one, the one Violet was talking about. He thought he finally knew why he felt like that oak tree in the meadow was special, because it really was.

Everyone except for Violet froze and reviewed the story. A clatter of shoes walked down the stones, Ewald and Alex directed their attention at him. Dhiman kept walking towards them, and squeezed himself between the two, pushing Alex away. The rest watched opened mouthed, surprised by his rudeness. "Hey, have you every heard about these two warlocks and a witch who vanquished an evil army" Ewald asked to find out extra information. Dhiman stared at him in an awkward look, "No not a thing" he lied. Then, he got up and went back away into the direction he came from. "What was that about?" Alex asked Ewald, "Not sure" he answered. "Hey, do you have a signal on your phone?" Ewald asked Alex, noticing that he left his at home. "No, why?" he asked back, "Oh, just wanted to do some research" he admitted. "What about the library?" he suggested as an alternative, "You know how this school is, one little thing and everybody is offended. The library barely has any exciting book, they wouldn't have one about an evil murderer," he said with a long sigh. Alex nodded his head agreeing with Ewald.

The two Selvins sat down on their soft beds facing each other. "Hey, could you..." Alex interrupted Ewald, "Check my phone?" he read his mind, Ewald nodded. Alex pulled his phone out of the cabinet between their two beds. He turned his large black phone on, tapping the screen a few times. "Yep, I got internet" he nearly cheered. "Okay, just let me, do this," he mumbled, "What do you want me to search?" he asked. "Uh search, major changing points in the magic section," he kindly ordered. Alex typed the phrase onto the screen, "Okay, look here" he said walking to Ewald's bed and showing him his new phone. They both read the shiny screen. 'The wonders of ancient Egypt' they read, "Hey once I heard that the only way the pyramids could have been built was by magic," he recalled passing on information that may not be true. "Oh" Ewald said trying to concentrate. 'The invention of the wand' they read, as he pushed the screen further down, 'The death of Peter' Alex thought as he reminded himself of all the stories his family would share about his great adventures. "Here" Ewald wailed with joy, making the boy in the next bed jump. "The fight of three" he added in a quieter voice. Alex tapped upon request and opened a black website. The title was in light grey and the following text in a contrasting white. "Hey, I don't feel like reading" Alex complained with a long whine, "Do you have the talk feature?" he asked hoping he knew what it is. "Oh" he remembered after a while of thinking.

It took a few seconds to start, but they were glad it did. "The fight of three" the soft female voice read the title of the page. "Once, there was an unappreciated man. As a child he had been abused and bullied" the voice paused. The boys already felt bad for him. "He grew jealous of other's lives, and needed something to achieve. He grew an army of vicious people, and decided one day to attack the people he hates and the parliament. Nearly a thousand joined, being promised wealth and a good life in the end" it stopped again. They just thought not even looking at the screen. "When things were at worst the three elders came to fight. They were so powerful that they could create almost anything. The two warlocks and witch stood in a meadow, waiting for the man who now called himself 'Gethin' to arrive with his army. It was a long battle, and then the three decided on an idea. They all centered all of their magic on Gethin's army. Most say that the army turned into a tree each soldier a leaf, and some believe that the tree attracts sorcerers thought's" Ewald grew a large smile. "But, the problem had not been solved, Gethin still remained. But, their powerful spells had a loophole. The three had drained all of their magic, saving us. They turned to stone each a different gem. Their descendant's found them, and swore to protect the gemstones. Gethin went back in hiding trying to rebuild his army," the voice chirped with a small robotic accent. The screen had a white flash as if a glitch, and then it restored the page. Alex looked down worried. "He also tried to undo the spell, it has been said that if he" the voice stopped in the middle of the sentence, slowly malfunctioning. Another flash came on, and the screen blacked out. Alex looked at Ewald frightened that his phone had broken. Then, lines of computer code ran from the bottom up, and they both suspected a virus at first. The long lights that hung from the ceiling flickered, as the phone shut off.

 They didn't say anything, as he panicked pressing the 'On' button. "You do know that was a hack?" Ewald asked in a shocked tone. His buddy stopped, understanding that it would never work. "So, that site was false?" he calmly replied, "It doesn't have to be the website, it could be someone who knows we're on it" Ewald said, both of them looking at the bedroom. Just for a quick second he had a suspicion that it had been Gethin himself, but he changed his mind and told his brain that it could have been a teacher. "Wait what did it say right before it cut off?" Alex asked in a happier voice. He thought without answering, "The website was just about to tell us how he could bring his army back" he answered his own question. "So, it's someone on his side trying to blind us" Alexander added even happier. Ewald closed his eyes for a while and yawned, "We'll find out tomorrow," he said indicating that he wanted to get some sleep. They both slipped under their warm covers and fell asleep.

Chapter 12

Winter's Break

The school stood at the foot of the first transporter, large yellow coats covering their usual uniforms. It was time to leave for break, and they were all waiting for their turns. One by one they would hop onto it and be put onto another on, by using their coordination's. Ewald's mother had not arranged any travel method that he could use, as he didn't know about any transporters lying around their home. After all the worry, Alex's family offered him to come over for the week.

    The two friends stood beside each other, they had no sight of Dhiman. They were near the beginning of the long unorganized crowd which was like a slow wave, pushing, wanting to return to their family and old friends. "You're gonna love it at our place" he said excited, referring to his house. Ewald only smiled, he wasn't too bright around people he never met before. "Oh well, thanks again for inviting me over" he replied in a ridiculous accent as if at a fancy hotel, just for a quick laugh. "Hey you know I have the funniest games" Alex added after he was done joking, "Most are violent" he warned with a tone that made him sound, not to care. Ewald shrugged moving up in the line. Although his mom wasn't a large fan of fighting games, it's not like she banned him from them. "Just a question, were do you keep your transporter?" Ewald asked him, "Oh, in our backyard" he answered in a split second. "Wouldn't other people see it?" he asked with curiosity, "Oh, its invisible until activated" Alex said after thinking. They stepped up to the transporter as Alex handed a round man his coordination. The man looked at it, rubbing his mustache. Then, he typed it onto a holographic projector. Alex and Ewald walked onto the transporter and vanished immediately.

    They stood on a miniscule blue platform, a beautiful garden around them. A row of multicolored roses outlined the wooden fence. Alex was glad to be back. Ewald on the other hand noticed no snow, "Isn't it winter?" he asked in a ridiculous tone, pointing at the yard. "No, we live more south" he explained. The two walked off of the transporter, and onto the red-bricked pathway that stroked through the grass. They passed around the petite tree, Alex rubbing it. "Okay, lets just pop inside" he muttered almost silently, at first Ewald had no idea what he meant but then it made sense. Alex opened the white backyard door just as big as needed, turned sideways, and walked into his house. As usual Ewald awkwardly followed him.

    The warm colors of their kitchen filled his eyes, yellows and oranges dominated the walls and furniture. Ewald already felt at home. To their right was a row of important appliances, with a small square table just for the three of them. The layout of the rooms appeared very simple. Large rooms with large openings, instead of doors. A long wide hallway stretched all the way to the door, as rooms hung in between. "So, where's your family?" Ewald asked eagerly, "Oh, here they come" he replied just noticing them climbing up from the garage. Two perfectly organized adults walked towards the two. The woman looking taller with her high black heels, as her tight brown skirt wrapped around her. Her hair neatly tucked in a ball, not even touching her white top. As for the man he wore a vertically striped suit, and slightly pointed shoes, he looked happier than ever to see his only son. "Dad, mom" Alex said looking at them. "How are you?" he asked his charming son, as the dad sped. "Great" he answered, as they both hugged him. "Oh, and you must be Ewald" the mother greeted him happily, her husband nodding. "So, how was Tralbon for the both of you?" he asked gazing at both of them. He himself had been taught at Tralbon, and he loved it. "It's fun" Ewald replied with an eruption, "Except for the work," Alex added to get a quick chuckle. "Well you two, I'll meet you back here for dinner," she said, walking towards the stove. "Let's get upstairs," Alex suggested trotting ahead. Ewald smiled and followed.

The rest of the afternoon the two explored Alex's room. They were talking and enjoying themselves, the time flew by like seconds. "Alex me and your father need to pick up some groceries, you know all the rules. Okay?" she announced up the complex stairs. The two walked out of his room, "Okay, Mrs. Egond" Ewald answered in a polite voice, trying to seem professional. Alex's parents walked out of the front door, as they ran down the stairs to the large plasma television. Alex cut through the kitchen and jumped into the living room. Ewald only slowly walked as if Alexander's parents were still watching.

Two hours passed, the boys were getting hungry and worried. Multiple possibilities ran through their heads as they watched reality television, injuries, accidents, kidnapping. Ewald stared at his best friend, "No" he said without knowing what he was going to say. "There is nothing wrong, they're just a little late," he added surprisingly he knew exactly what Ewald was thinking of. "Sure" he said, "Maybe they just won the lottery, and they're off spending it on Christmas presents and chocolate" Ewald added, trying to change their minds. Alex tried to watch TV, but the ideas still came back. "But, they would tell us. At least call us," he said frustrated. Ewald just thought for two minutes, "Should we call the police?" he asked still trying to process the show. Alex shook his head hesitantly, "We can't call, what if they walk in right after?" "It's better not to do anything," he added. Their worrying grew every second, as they watched they got new ideas that horrified them.

A long time passed before the phone finally rang, Alex leaped towards it. "Hello" he said rushing the grey object up to his ear. Ewald staring as he waited, all that he could hear was mumbling on the other side of the phone. "Wait where you are?" Alexander asked not knowing, another sentence of whispering filled Ewald's ear. He disappointedly pushed the phone away. "So, where are they?" he asked his friend, "He didn't say" Alex sighed. "But, at least we know that they're safe" he added on a lighter note. Ewald smiled, now he could return to thinking about the three gems, and how Gethin could bring his army back. "So, Gethin" he said plainly, knowing that Alex would understand. "I still can't figure it out, I've been searching everything" he notified him, Ewald in fact had not done any research, and he was still trying to comprehend the whole story. "Too bad" he replied to his comment. "You know, we could look through some of my dad's files" Alex said jumping from the black leather couch. "He has historical documents?" Ewald said wanting to verify, he only nodded. "Well then, let's go" Ewald yelped standing beside Alex.

Side by side the two ran to a closet, Alex pulling out a thick brown business binder. They jogged back into the living room, and spread the files onto the carpeted ground. Ewald started rummaging back and forth through the piles of paper, some papers were whiter then possible, but some looked very antique and scratched. "Are you sure your dad is okay with us looking through this stuff?" Ewald asked about the important information. Alex didn't reply right away, he was first thinking of the consequences of his decision. He looked up at Ewald's worried face, "Yep, he'll be all right with it," he said quickly. They turned their heads back down at the papers, flipping through files, only glancing at a couple of words.

"Hey, your dad is a lawyer?" he asked holding up an official certificate, "Uh, yeah" he answered not resting from searching. The two explored more and more papers, each time finding extra information about the magic section, but they still have not come across any papers about a large fight. Ewald stopped to think once, but without a word continued.

Time passed as the two looked for the information. "I found something about a gem" Alex interrupted in a voice unsure if it was what they were looking for. He held up a file, with a large italic title. "Good" he said relieved of the fact that he didn't have to look anymore. Ewald gently grabbed it from his hand; he stared at it for a couple of seconds then began to read. "Only one gem had been revealed to our sources. It lies inside of the... family" he stopped for Alex. "But, currently it had not been sighted, and they have not confirmed any facts" he finished off. "What a waste of paper" Mr. Egond said trying to lighten the day; Ewald gave him a nasty look. "It doesn't even tell us whose family it is the writing is smudged" Ewald added. Alex opened his mouth to speak, but before he could the doorbell rang, and the door unlocked.

He automatically knew that his parents had finally arrived. They both jumped up to greet his family, running up to the front door. It opened revealing his father, and his mother with a blanket in her hands. "Dad, I thought something bad happened to you" Alexander shouted happily, "No, it was something good" he confirmed. Alex thought, "What?" he asked in a lower voice. Mrs. Egond smiled excited, "You have a baby sister" the words exploded from inside her mouth. Ewald hopped, as his friend laughed with joy. Even a few tears filled his large eyes, as he chuckled. "Can I see her?" he asked in a watery tone even though he knew the answer was yes. The mother handed Alex his new sister, wrapped in a pink blanket, which covered her green baby clothing. Her blue eyes sparkled in the sunlight that was leaking in through the door, as her soft pink lips sat below her tiny nostrils. "What's her name?" Ewald asked as Alex looked upwards at his mother. She looked at here husband who was still beside her, "She's Helen" he said to the kids. "Aw, she's so cute" Alex pointed out, "Alex, how about I take Helen upstairs and you can see her later" she suggested, as Alex gave her his new baby sister. Mr. Egond followed his wife to their bedroom, talking with excitement. "So far, your house is great. Just like you said" Ewald thanked.

Two weeks had passed and it was Christmas morning. Ewald woke up to the sound of Alex singing joyfully inside the bathroom next door to their guest room. He opened his eyes, as the light brown paint rushed to his brain. Ewald looked around silently, over the past week and a half he had learned to call this room his temporary home. He slid his feet off of the side of the bed, as he straightened his back. He had wondered if he would or would not receive any presents from Alex's parents, as a guest he felt too shy to ask them over break. He hopped onto his skinny feet, and walked towards the door. Alex jumped out of the bathroom and scared Ewald. "Merry Christmas" he shouted, Ewald jumped back. "Wait, I don't celebrate Christmas," he recalled. Alex stared at him surprised, "Why?" He looked up at him, "My birthday is the day right after Christmas, and I suggested that my family only celebrate it" he answered in a shy voice. To Alex that sounded conceded, but Ewald had nothing to do with the decision. It was actually the fact that his mother was running low on money, and did not think it would help her financially. "Well, you can still get a present for your birthday" he reassured him, knowing that he still wanted to receive one.

They both ran down the stairs happily, and walked to the neat kitchen. Mrs. and Mr. Egond were cooking a breakfast for the whole family and Ewald. "There you are," she said hugging Alex and smiling at Ewald, "We've cooked a special breakfast for the two of you" the father said. Only now had the scent of toast and fresh eggs reached their noses. "But first, your presents" the dad read both of their minds, as his mother grabbed two large presents out of a white cupboard. "One for you" she muttered with a smile, as she handed a present over to her son. "And, one for you" she added tossing the second large present to Ewald. "Thank you," he replied with red cheeks. Alex paused, "Where is Helen?" he said awkwardly as he had never said that sentence before. "She is upstairs sleeping" Mr. Egond pointed out, barely moving his mouth. Alex sighed longing to see his sister again. "Listen we'll all eat breakfast, then you can open your presents" the mom suggested to them. Ewald and Alex nodded, looking over at the table, it looked flooded with food. Alex's mouth watered as he saw his favorite foods. They quickly sat down and began eating.

Alex like always finished before anyone else, he was really looking forward to opening his Christmas present. After his best friend had finished, he ripped off the wrapping paper. Alex stared at it for a couple of seconds, and then smiled. Ewald glanced over; he was holding the new multiple vehicle package. It was a car that could open up its wings and fly, and then land onto water. Alex had been begging his parents for one all of last summer. Then, he looked back at his own gift. He was unwrapping it slowly; the parents watched waiting to see his expression. "Alex told us how much you loved reading, so we decided this was the best present" the dad said, almost thanking his son. He loved it; all of the best books tied together, most of them he actually really wanted to read. He kept glancing back and forth between the colorful and bright books. "Thank You, I really do love this birthday present," he said standing up from the ground. "You're welcome" Alex's mother said, "You have fun" her husband added. The two walked in a professional way, with their chins pointing up.

They spent the rest of the day playing in the backyard, making the transforming vehicle fly and dive into their mini pond. This truly was one of Ewald's favorite days.

"Ewald, when does school start?" Alex asked as the sun began to set. He thought back to their schedule, "Tomorrow" he shouted slightly unhappy. "And, when do we have to leave?" he asked another question, "Now" he added. The two jumped off of the bench, and ran inside through the open door. They jogged into their room, and grabbed their belongings and presents out of the white closets. In a hurry they said goodbye to Alex's parents, and rushed back out into the dark backyard. They stopped to breath, they were now both drenched in sweat. "Time to leave" Alex spoke for Ewald, "Yep" he replied in a sadder tone. Alex pulled out a pink paper, and punched in Tralbon's coordination. Together they stepped onto the transporter, and they flashed out of sight.

Chapter 13

The Secret Code

Amazingly it was light outside, and it looked as if still the afternoon. They both assumed that the two places were in two different time zones. Also unlike his house, snow covered the once green landscape. Ewald frowned, he was just getting used to the nice warmer weather and the lively grass. Ewald jumped off, his shoes sinking two inches. Alex followed with the exact same movement. "Let's go this way" Ewald motioned towards the edge of the forest that touched the tall hedges. "Okay" his friend excitedly answered, speed walking over by his side. A couple of floating clouds ran in front of the sun, as the two walked into the small pathway that led to the silver entrance. They both grew smirks on their faces, the second they caught a glance of the sparkling object. It reminded them of how they had gotten here, and all the fun that they had had. Deep inside the fog there was a problem, suddenly the two weren't as happy. Alex held up a security stick that one of the teachers had given them, and just as it was supposed to the gate opened. They now had a better view. Teachers and students gathered around an empty circle, they were all standing around the old site of the lion fountain.

Ewald at first didn't believe his eyes, but as they stepped towards the group he understood. Alex gazed over at his best friend to read his expressions, only shock on his face. They both learned to expect the worst, but the worst is not always the truth. The talking group in front of them looked at them, as if they had to blame for this. "What happened?" Alex asked, he thought that the question would make them stop staring. "We don't know" a short woman wearing a plaid dress answered, "Yesterday it was here, now it's not," she continued in an Irish accent. Ewald shrugged without getting asked a single thing.

"Are there any marks?" he asked from the pressure of having to talk. "What?" the same woman asked "Marks, like a truck" he clarified. She pointed with her thick finger at the ground, looking straight at him. Ewald felt like everyone was against him. "Let's go find Professor Hegnorf" Alex said, as they walked past the crowd and up the tower steps.

They quickly scurried up the elevator and into the hexagonal room. Alex froze just as he saw his favorite teacher. "Hello, how are you?" their professor greeted them, although he was mainly directing his welcome towards Alex. "Great" Ewald answered only seconds after the question. Alex stopped to think, "You know that the lion fountain is missing, right?" he asked. Professor Hegnorf shot a look back at him, as if thinking that he could have stolen it. "Well, of course I know. Teachers are allowed to stay at Tralbon, in fact most of them did," he answered adding extra information. Just before Alex was about to ask again Ewald talked, "What do you think happened?" he blurted kindly. "Most teachers say it's been stolen" he said closing his eyes for a few seconds, "And you think?" Alex added. "I don't think I should tell you this, it may..." he paused, "It may frighten you," he said looking back and forth between the two students. Alex nodded as if approving the idea. "Have any of you heard the story of Gethin?" he asked in a weird tone, they looked at each other nodding. "Well, some say that he stole it.

[106]

Well actually not some, only I think that" he informed them. They all stood to think, "Why do you think that?" Ewald asked curiously, "What's so special about the fountain?" Alexander asked adding onto his friend's question. "Really the only special thing about that fountain is the writing" he answered, "The language that it was written in is far extinct, and you really have to examine it. But, there is a way to solve it in fact I did, three years ago" he taught his best students. "What does it say?" they asked him at the same time. "It lies up high near the beginning" the teacher answered in a mystical voice. "Thanks" Ewald said grabbing Alex's hand, as he ran into the north.

As they ran through the dark tunnel, he began to loosen his grip of his hand. Alex pushed on the Selvin door, and it swung open. They jogged their way up the stairs and landed on their beds. Ewald sat for a minute to catch his breathe, "So, what does the riddle mean?" Alex asked. "It lies up high near the beginning" Ewald repeated to remind the two. They stopped, "Where? Where is the beginning?" he asked in a whisper. "Where did we come from?" Alex asked although he already knew the answer. "Drolers, so what Gethin wants is inside Drolers" Ewald said, feeling like a detective. "And what Gethin wants are the Gems. One of the gems is inside the hospital," Alex added to what his friend had said. They thought about the other half of the message, "Up high?" he asked himself. "Maybe its behind the large clock"

Alex suggested it as the answer. Ewald still unhappy with the answer kept thinking, "Up high, up high" he mumbled. "Wait what about near the moving hospital beds. Remember the archway with the huge blue stone at the top?" he asked his buddy, sure that he would agree. "Ya, I guess," he answered still preferring his answer. "We have to go save it from him" he said feeling heroic. "But, how do we get there?" Ewald asked, "I have a book with all the coordination of public places inside the magic section" Alex reminded him. "Grab the book, and then we'll go back down to the transporter" he ordered in a friendly way.

Alex pulled out and wore a brown bag, as Ewald ran down the stairs to the warm lounge. He walked out of the large door, staring through the long tunnel into the crystal ball room, trying to see if he could spot their professor but he was long out of sight. His friend came out with the backpack over his shoulders, "Let's go this way," Alex suggested pointing to the glass elevator, which was blocked by a brick door that almost seemed invisible. "Sure" his best friend followed, they stood in front of the wall and it opened. Ewald stepped away, he wasn't too happy about riding up so high. Alex stepped into the half circle, motioning Ewald in. After he entered it closed, and slowly moved along the brick outside of the school.

They both exited the glass structure at the same time. Far off Ewald could see the 'Forest of Charms' and the lake that Sophie had fallen into. The two continued straight towards the bright blue transporter. On their way Alex was opening the book and searching for the coordination. Ewald glanced to his left and noticed that a coordination book was just like a phone book. "Hospitals, hospitals, hospitals" Alex muttered looking for Drolers, "Oh here it is" pointing it out for Ewald to see. It looked almost identical to latitude and longitude; just extra numbers were added to the end. Almost like a password so not just anyone with a transporter can enter into your house. When they reached the object, Alex ran over to the side to enter the numbers. Then, together they jumped on with force, flashed blue, and disappeared.

White bricks flashed around them, only now had Ewald remembered how bright Drolers' walls were. At first the two didn't realize were they had been put, but they both understood now. The Drolers transporter was at the back of the eating area, although now none of the tables were there. They stepped off of the blue object. "First, we'll check the clock" Alex commanded pointing at the large black antique clock, which hung over the entrance to the staircase. Ewald quietly sighed, he was still sure that it was not hidden behind it. "But, how are you going to check?" he asked as he walked behind Alex, "I'll use the x-ray stick charm" he showed off, smirking at his face. He pulled out his short wand, pointing it at the clock. Alex thought of the result and in seconds he had x-ray vision of what he was pointing at. His smile turned to a frown, as he couldn't find a single clue, "Nope" he said, making Ewald even surer that it was on top of the arch. "Well come on" Alex muttered at him, as they both walked up the stairs. Ewald and Alex turned left into a long empty hallway, walking faster every second. They really needed to see it, meanwhile inside their heads they were thinking of plans to hide the gem. For once Ewald thought of stealing, but it would be for the better. Alex turned right signaling Ewald through the archway. A room filled with hospital beds, with another room behind, confronted them both. "So, how are we going to save it?" Ewald asked, as he turned to look at the large blue topaz. "Oh my god, where is it?" Alex said horrified, his best friend didn't reply, his mouth was wide open of surprise. Ewald looked at Alex, "Do you think he took it?" he asked. He only nodded, not wanting to say a word.

 Scaring the two old boys, a man popped his head through the left side of the door. His appearance was slightly scary. He had pure white hair that looked like spikes coming out from his head. Large round glasses covered his eyes; he seemed quite secretive, as the glasses were pitch black. He wore a small smile, it didn't mean that he was happy, maybe amused. The strange-outfitted man stepped out, revealing the rest of his body. "Is that a leather jacket?" Alex rudely whispered as he stepped backwards, the man shot a nasty look at the student. The man approached the boys as they walked away in fear. His smile grew as they grew more scared. "I've heard, you know a thing or two about the Gems of Time," he said in a deep French accent. "Are you Gethin?" Alex asked almost whimpering. The man looked at him, quickly his smile dropped. They were waiting for a reply, but he said not a word. "This one is gone" he reassured them, every second they were getting more and more convinced that the man with the darkened glasses was Gethin. He paused wanting to sound dramatic, "Two remain," he said. Ewald turned to look at Alex. "It's before Drolers," he added mysteriously. Without another word he was out of the room, running back down the hall.

The boys froze still scared by the odd man. "We better get back to my house" Ewald reminded him, "Wait, who said it was at your house?" he asked. "Well, he was looking at me, when he said it" he said back at him. "Well, my dad knows a thing or two about history" he claimed. Ewald looked at him with honest eyes, "Sure, we'll go to you house" Alex said slightly looking forward to entering his house. "Let's go back to Tralbon" Ewald said in a happier voice,

"Okay," he whispered. They walked slower than before. They both relaxed that they didn't have to steal the gem to protect it, but they were worried that Gethin may once again rule.

Chapter 14

Going Back

It had been a week since the two boys had come back from Drolers. The entire week they had been searching for a way to get to his house. Alex then found the phone number of Ewald's young aunt, and got an extra pair of keys to their house.

"How again are we going to get to my house?" he asked as he fixed his bed. "Well, I was thinking of using the... um..." Alex said frustrating him. "How about we fly?" Ewald joked, he only stared thinking, "Okay." "What? I was kidding" he said surprised that he had agreed to his ridiculous plan. "We can grow wings and fly there" he repeated, "No, no, I am not flying" he stressed to him. "Why? Just try it" Alex urged, Ewald continued without saying anything. "Come on" he said pointing with his left hand at the staircase.

The two plopped down from the staircase that led outside from Professor Selvia's room. "We're first going to transport to my house, then fly to yours, 'cuz it's faster" he informed him although he already knew. They both ran to the blue transporter, Ewald this time typed in the coordination. Together they stepped onto the object and flashed away. The same garden appeared, the two smiled, feeling the warm air. The sweet scent of cut grass filled their nostrils; they relaxed as the sun warmed their frozen cheeks. "Let's fly" Alex said in a dramatic voice.

"See this?" Alex asked holding up a mucus green bottle, he only nodded knowing that he had to drink the liquid. "My parents gave this to me only for emergencies, and the world getting destroyed is defiantly an emergency" he added. "This liquid, if you drink it you will grow wings, just like a large fairy"

Alex told him, "Great, I've always wanted to be a fairy" Ewald said sarcastically. Alex stared trying to convince him that this was a big deal. "Okay, so you take a sip then I will," he commanded handing over the clear bottle. Ewald took off the brown cork at the top, sniffing it he groaned. "Uh, yuck. This smells terrible" he complained, "Just drink it, remember the gems" his friend encouraged. "You cheering won't help" he joked, slightly frustrating him. "Sure" he said, a second before he took a long drink. His eyes nearly jumped from the sourness of the liquid, he finally pulled back. "That was just gross" Ewald said, handing over the slightly full container. Alex rubbed the top with his sleeve, thinking that it would remove the bacteria. Lifting it up to his mouth he drank, his reaction was less immerse as the other one. "Hey, where are our wings?" Ewald asked confused. He did not reply, only shrugging notifying him that he had not a clue. Then, both of their backs felt a strange tickle, followed by a small burn. Suddenly, out of nowhere a set of white feathery wings jumped out, ripping their shirts.

"Wow" they both exclaimed. "This is amazing" Ewald said seeing this for the first time. "Great now I can't put on by bag" Alex informed Ewald, "Just carry it." "Yeah, time to teach you to fly" he said excited, waiting to see Ewald's failed attempt. He shook his legs as if preparing. "So, first you jump" Alexander guided, demonstrating in slow motion.

"Next, you imagine that you are floating" he ordered, as he jumped, closed his eyes, and amazingly floated. Ewald tried once only falling onto his face, but the second time he was just as high as Alex. "Okay, now this is the hard part. We need to move our wings" he paused to think of the best way to explain it. "First, you pop your chest outwards" he said as they both followed his instructions. "Now, individually imagine the wing flapping. Once, you do it once or twice you will continue to move" he instructed, and within seconds Alex was flying in circles. "Try it," he said, Ewald pressed against his shoulders and thought about them moving. Amazingly Ewald began to fly around, "Did you do this before?" Alexander asked, lying, as it was very easy to see that he had no practice. Ewald silently thanked him, "Do you have the map?" he asked concerned. "Here it is," he answered pulling it out of his tight pocket, a modern colored map shone under the bright sun. "Well, let's fly" Ewald said excited and scared.

The first fifteen minutes were beautiful; the two would gaze down and look at the nice green landscape. Afterwards they both got bored, and their backs hurt. They tried to pass their time by playing games and solving riddles, but they still weren't as happy. "Okay we're here," he told Ewald, who looked like he was about to fall asleep. "Now, just imagine stopping your wings, not the actual levitating, or you will go falling down" he warned. Alexander first stopped moving, but still floating on air. "Your turn" Alex encouraged, and just as he had done Ewald copied. "Now we just need to glide downwards" he said, not giving his friend enough information, but even without anything to follow he made it. They touched the ground of the grey sidewalk, first their toes then resting back. Just like the wings had grown out they shrunk disappearing, but this time they did not feel it. "I'm home" Ewald sighed happily, Alex a little disappointed smiled. They stood for a minute, and then Ewald welcomed him as they opened the door. Only a second of happiness remained, before they understood what they saw. The worst tragedy that had happened to Ewald since his dad had died was sitting before his eyes. His house was wrecked.

This was not the kind of wrecked you might think, nothing was standing except the bricks. The boys said not a word, knowing that if they did they would just make it worst. Ewald stepped into his used to be home, everything turned upside down. The partly ash covered floorboards creaked as he rested his foot on them. He looked over at the stairs; even the soft vanilla carpet was ripped off. Today couldn't get worse, even for Alex. A few tears rolled down Ewald's cheek, trying to hide it from his friend he walked in further. They passed the main washroom; he did not dare look inside it. The kitchen table was in ruins on the ground, the chairs around it blow into a million pieces. Then only one thing caught

Alexander's eye, he stopped directing Ewald to it. Their hearts nearly stopped looking at a large circular shape it the wall, they both knew that he had visited, Gethin had been here. They kept staring at it, imagining him rummaging through his house looking for a gem.

"So, he was here" Alex said referring to Gethin. His friend did not answer, only nodding to verify that he had heard. He stood feeling dead in the gut, Ewald only thought about what had happened to the gem, if he had found it or not.

"Mom" he quickly shouted scaring Alex. As they ran he looked around nervously, he had already lost one of his parents, losing another would be tragic. He began weeping as he ran up the stairs, "Mom" he repeated this time sobbing harder. Alexander followed trying not to get in his way, he was never good with dealing with emotions, especially not other's. "Ewald" he heard a faint voice say, he began running faster towards his mother's bedroom. A yellow room came up as they opened its door, "Mom" he said again worried that he would find Gethin. The two slowed down relieved to find only Mrs. Ellington, she was crying at the foot of her broken dark brown bed. She looked up at the boys, standing up embarrassed. "Ewald" she said trying to explain to him as they hugged. "Did he get the gem?" he asked surprising her, "What?" she asked amazed that he had figured out. "Gethin... did he get it?" He repeated, "No, he didn't" she answered in a dreadful way. Only a part of the boys cheered up, "So, he didn't find it" he wanted to confirm, "Nope" his mother answered glancing at Alex. "Hello, you must be Ewald's friend" she greeted; it was the first time she had said that phrase. "Hi, I'm Alexander" he replied using his full name, "I'm so sorry about" he said before she cut him off. "Oh, don't be that sorry" she said confusing them, "The world is fine, I still have the gem." Alex looked over at Ewald, "No, I was talking about the house" Alex said pointing around. His mother tried to smile but it didn't seem to work, "Oh, well that's not too bad" she said trying not to hurt her son's feelings. "The magic section is replacing this house with another, for free" she looked at Ewald, waiting to see his expression. No one said a word after that for two whole minutes.

"Listen boys" she nicely commanded, "You two go back to school, they'll repair this house, and everything will be fine" Ewald's mother assured them. "Okay" Alex thought, "But what about the other gem, there is another one left, right?" He asked. "Maybe, unless he got it by now" she muttered, as she pulled her spine up. Ewald walked away although he didn't want his mother to get hurt. "Oh, mom..." he quietly shouted, "be careful." The boys turned around and walked through the small hallway, "Oh, we have a transporter in the yard now" she informed them, yelling at the top of her lungs. Without thinking they dragged themselves down the stairs, through the broken door and into the yard. Pulling their things onto the transporter, Alexander opened his book typing in the code. They flashed away, as his mother watched through the upstairs chattered window.

Stepping off of the transporter and onto the Tralbon grass, they turned to face each other. "Are we going to go after the last gem?" Alex asked tired. It took him a while to think, "How about we try stay away from trouble this time" Ewald answered not feeling in the mood for looking for another shiny stone.

That very night everyone was in bed. Alex was already completely snoring, just like almost all of the other Selvin males. Ewald's back slumped on the bed, he couldn't get to sleep. The whole time he was having flashbacks of his house and of how his mother was going to spend the next few days. He silently sat playing with his thumbs to pass the time, even if he forced himself to try to sleep, it would have never worked.

Chapter 15

The Third Stone

Alexander continuously tapped on the screen of the food selector, he had been pressing on the cheese omelet option and it would only give him a cherry pie. He banged with the bottom of his fist as if demanding the machine to take it back. "Here I'll take the pie, and you can have my omelet" Ewald suggested walking over to his dear friend. He smiled, because in fact Alex was waiting for him to trade the entire time. "Thanks" he said taking the white plate from his tray. They walked over to an empty table, and ate in peace. Until a thin handsome student who looked a few years older than the two poked their backs. Ewald turned around but Alex didn't seem to bother, he just continued chewing. "Have you heard the news?" he asked quickly, "News?" Ewald replied really not caring. "Here" he shouted, throwing a newspaper across, almost hitting his pie. The boy waited for him to pick it up, and then trotted away to the next group of people. "What's that?" Alex asked looking over his shoulder, "I don't know" Ewald answered still reading the headlines on the first page. "Something about a..." he said pausing, "Gem" Alexander shouted, reading ahead. They turned to each other exchanging concerned looks, "Only one is left" Ewald muttered, feeling worried about his mother. Alex tossed the bundle of paper on the other side of the table, not wanting to read anymore. Ewald stared at his watch recalling the time they had to be in history class, "We need to go" he told him. They both got up and walked up to the speedy elevator, without cleaning up their table.

The boys zipped upwards, Alexander whistling nervously. Ewald didn't know why he was whistling but he always loved to listen to classical music. The room stopped moving; they shoved the door open and walked to the crystal ball room. The students turned right into the South tunnel, awkwardly walking. They opened the antique wooden door, and climbing into the left path. They entered the history classroom, in which they had the Halloween Hunt. The class was different; all of the desks and chairs had been pushed to the sides. They were stacked in an organized manner. At first they didn't recognize the tall man in front of the class setting up an old film projector, but they realized that he had been the man who had howled at Professor Hegnorf, the day he set the class on fire. Although they knew that it was an accident, it was still very serious. He looked much happier this time, "Oh, hello" he said directed to the shy students. A couple of girls walked up behind them, trying to push them through. The teacher continued smiling, nodding at each student who entered. "Just sit down," he kindly ordered after half of the class had arrived. They sat down realizing that they would be watching an educational film. Alexander frowned; he wasn't in the mood to watch an old movie. After the students made rows, the professor started the black and white film.

The title "RMS Titanic" flashed across the screen, Ewald didn't like it so far. He was never into events like that, and he knew that this was to honor the day that it had collided with the iceberg. The screen turned clockwise, it was the worst effect that they had seen in a movie, but in fact back then this was the coolest. "In the beginning, they created three..." the male narrator said, as the screen showed blueprints, sketches, and design ideas to the camera. "Their names were Titanic, Olympic, and Britannic," he continued. All of the students were comfortable, and begun to quiet down. It was five minutes into the film, both of the boys were already bored and they had heard that this was a two hour-long movie. Then, a loud boom sounded from the door, as their shy Professor Hegnorf walked in. He waved at Alex and looked back up. With silence he walked over to the side, leaning over to their teacher. He whispered as Alexander watched, trying to read their lips. They spent about another two minutes talking back and forth, by now Alex heard nothing but their voices. He concentrated on listening, he would always love to hear gossip and rumors, but he never spread them around.

For a few seconds he understood nothing but then it all translated. "It's been stolen" their new teacher repeated in shock, "Yes, and he has also taken the other one" Professor Hegnorf added. Alex's heart plummeted downwards, now all what stood between the world turning upside down is Ewald's mother. "Who had it?" the history teacher asked in an excited voice. "Mr. Hullog" he answered after he had thought. He looked away from the conversation; Alex did not need any more information. He shifted his legs to get into his pocket; Alex reached in to pull out his phone. Luckily, he got it fixed over Christmas break, when he went back home. Alexander turned it on, hiding it using his hands. Ewald looked over to his left and pretended that he had never seen anything. Alex opened the Internet, opening his dad's website. He had seen his dad's password over the break. A professionally designed site opened as a list of names and dates opened up. He clicked his phone to scroll to the H's. After minutes of searching he found, "Mr. Rick Hullog." He clicked on the link anxious to see the information. A list of data appeared all in a maroon red. Alex read through the words, it was hard to concentrate with an annoying voice showing you the Titanic. "Hey, do you know what this has to do with magic?" Ewald asked not even looking in his direction. "Maybe, they used it to build the ship," he said, not knowing. "Okay class, time is up," said the professor who had still not taught them his name. Alexander jumped scared; he had spent the whole class researching Mr. Hullog. "We'll finish the rest of the film next class," he told them, as he pressed the antique pause button. All the students stood up, stretching their sore legs. After the students had moved out of the way, the teacher pointed at the two side piles of furniture, closed his eyes and pulled his hand inwards. In a few seconds the items were floating in slow motion, returning to their usual positions. They silently watched then left the room.

The students continued to the trapezoid room, and turned into the tunnel leading to the magical creatures' classroom. "Hey" Alex said as he pulled Ewald from the rest of the group, "I need to tell you something" he added frantic. He walked pulling him by the sleeve, "Where are we going" Ewald asked worried that something had happened. "Oh, we're going to the Selvin room" Alex answered as he let go of him. The boys entered the long room, and climbed up the boy's staircase. At the same time they jumped onto each of their beds. They said nothing for a while, "What about class?" He asked, not wanting to get in trouble. "Just skip it," he answered without any care. Alex stopped to think of what he would say next, "Listen, the third gem has been stolen" he re informed his roommate. "Your mom has the very last one," he recalled. They thought for a quick second, "What do we do?" Ewald asked. "Here is the plan, tomorrow we rush over to your house..." he begun to answer before he was interrupted, "Tomorrow is the last soccer tournament of the year, and they'll be checking every person in" he reminded him. Alex groaned, by then Gethin would have definitely gotten the last gem of time. "Fine we'll go after the stupid soccer competition" he whined as he gave in to Ewald. "So, now what?" He asked Alex, "I heard that the creatures' class is inside today," he said. "So?" Ewald asked, he did not understand how it had solved his problem. "So, now we can go to the forest, haven't you ever wondered what is behind the archway and the path?" He asked, trying to convince Ewald of coming with him. Ewald thought, he in fact did want to go through the arch, "Well..." he said. "Just come on" Alex encouraged although it sounded more like a command.

They jumped down the stairs of the East tower. They looked back upon the place of which the fountain had been; to the two the idea of Gethin keeping the lion fountain was just unfair. They walked through the small opening; they both carefully checked that the class was not outside. Still silent, Alexander led his worried friend. The boys trotted past the miniature lake, as they searched for the antique archway. None of them could find it. All that Ewald could see were trees, and Alex continued walking back and forth in the spot he thought that it should be in. "I know, it was here" Alex said, standing on top of his best guess. Ewald did not reply, "I can't even see the path, so Gethin couldn't have stolen them," he added trying to outsmart Ewald. "I... I don't know," he admitted even thought he had not asked a question. They simply stood to think; nothing different came to mind except for Gethin, and the Gems of Time. "Okay, here is what we do" Ewald said, as he tried to lead them back on track. "We can just go back to the Selvin room, then when the next class is about to start we blend in with the others," he added, wanting to avoid trouble. "Sure" his friend said in a desperate tone, and together they ran to the elevator on the end of the sorting room.

Chapter 16
A Problem Rises

Ewald smiled at the crack of dawn, he was excited for the tournament. The night before; the students had bought face paint and colored themselves. All the Selvins colored themselves red, unlike the Katnors who painted blue stripes underneath their eyes. A nice beginning of April breeze flew in from the slightly opened window. Ewald rose from his messy bed, he was still rubbing his eyes because of the fact that yesterday he couldn't get any sleep. As he moved away from his bed he noticed that all the others were gone except for Alexander. Ewald walked and shook his body, trying to wake Alex up. "Ugh" Alex groaned, as he pulled back his saliva from his chin. "What?" He asked, still half asleep. "Don't you remember what today is?" he asked happily, "Is it the hotdog eating contest? " he asked as a joke. Ewald smirked, "Just get up," he said pulling him up by the hand. "The soccer tournament, is it today?" He reminded himself as he got off of the bed. His friend only nodded his head, "Well it's a good thing we're not competing," he said sounding slightly a bit happier. "I'm going to go to the south bathroom" Alexander informed Ewald, just in case he needed him with something. "Okay" he hollered to Alex, who was now half way down the steps. "Just don't rub off all the red paint," he reminded him, Alex didn't reply.

Time passed as Ewald made both his and Alex's beds, finally he had come back. "Wow, you look happy" Ewald remarked, glancing over at Alex with the corner of his eye. "Yeah" he confirmed, "Did someone flood the toilet again?" He asked, knowing that it had made him smile before. "No" he said in a mean voice, "Someone flooded all the toilets" he told letting out the biggest laugh in the world. Ewald looked at him concerned, "And the best part is, the custodian had to clean it up" Alex said letting out even more laughter. "Poor Mr. Mart" his friend said, feeling bad for the janitor. "More like Mr. Fart" he joked, "That's not funny" Ewald taught his buddy, putting him down. "Come on, let's go outside" Alex said, disappointed that he did not like the pun. Together they proceeded towards the half circle glass elevator. It opened as the beautiful view flew into their eyes, it was amazing. Tall silver bleachers stood on two sides of soccer field; the view of line after line of people was just magnificent. They exited, "Let's go get a good spot," Ewald told Alex. "Hi" Dhiman surprised them, Ewald smiled at him while Alex frowned. They began walking towards the bleachers when the tall blonde woman from the Halloween Hunt stopped them. "Oh, hello boys" she said glancing at the three, "You need to go through the short cut" she informed them as the teacher pointed at the blue transporter beside the fenced in area. Ewald smiled, "Thank You" he thanked.

  He continued staring at her, something about her was not right. Without seeing where he was going he tripped on a large rock. Ewald collapsed on the ground, thankfully his hands helped land him softer. The two haters that were walking beside him had not noticed that he had fallen because they were too busy arguing. Ewald stood up patting his clothing to get rid of the dirt. Alex and Dhiman together vanished, Ewald turned to look at the other transporter, and the two had safely gotten to the other side. Finally, Alexander noticed and waited for Ewald to catch up. He watched him disappear, but nothing came out form the other side. "Hey, it shouldn't take that long" Dhiman said, very worried. "Even for a full class that's too long" he added annoyingly. "I know!" Alexander screamed as loud as he could. Everyone around looked at the two, judging them without knowing the problem. Alex wanted to apologies, but half of him felt that he deserved it. The two continued standing there, their faces completely red.

A dark background moved in, as Ewald flashed away. Minimal light was leaking through the extensive amount of trees. They were tall and eerie, for only one thought he suggested that this was Tralbon's Forest of Charms, yet again the trees in that forest had no resemblance. He stood in an opening, the dusty dirt along the ground. Three short pillars stood in front of him, the white statues looked as if they could have been taken straight out of a museum. "Where am I?" Ewald asked himself in only a whisper, as he was afraid that a wild animal might track him down. He heard only the sound of his breath, as his lungs begun to quicken. "Oh" an old voice sighed, "Why? Don't you know?" It asked even louder. Ewald jumped off of the mini transporter, he shook as if he had just finished swimming in the Arctic Ocean. "You don't even know your own school," he said with a chuckle, "This is the other side of the forest," he informed him. He did not reply to that, "Who are you?" Ewald asked frightened that he might hurt him. "Oh, so you haven't heard of me" he said slightly mad, "Maybe these will remind you" he continued in an even heavier tone. Two stones flew out of nowhere; they stopped to levitate over the right and left pillars. On his left was the one from Drolers, on the other pillar floated the one that Mr. Hullog must have been hiding.

Ewald felt the danger grow; he was standing near a man who had killed hundreds of people. "Gethin" he whimpered, "So, you are Ewald" he sighed in relief that it was the right boy. He nervously looked around; the worst possible thing is to not know where someone is. "Where are you?" He asked, really wanting to know. A quick movement slid across the trees, as Gethin emerged from beside the pillar to Ewald's left. At first the view was terrible but as he came out into the opening it became clearer. His long black robe with a hood stretched past his feet. Ewald grew more scared by the second, what would he do to him. Gethin stood still for a minute, pointing his head to the ground. Then, with a rush he pulled his head back, nothing was there. Nothing was between the hood and the robe, nothing except two beady blue eyes. The rest of the hood must be blocking the light from above, Ewald tried to reassure himself. "So, you know what I'm after, right?" he asked, as his eyes grew bigger. "The gems" Ewald muttered. Gethin only nodded, as his hood and eyes jumped. "I've gotten two," he said in a creepy voice, "And, you are my weapon to the third, the emerald" he said with a cold laugh. Gethin swung his arm, pointing over behind the trees, quickly and suddenly the cage fell around the standing Ewald. "I've caught you now" he remarked with a sneer.

Ewald sat down on the dirty ground, he had just wanted to watch the game and now an evil army leader was capturing him. The silver cage looked much like a birdcage with a rounded top, now Ewald actually understood how bad a cage really is. "Listen, I don't know where you got the information that I have the last Gem of Time, but I don't have it" Ewald said standing up for himself. "Oh, I know that your mother has it" he informed him, correcting his thoughts about the plan. "You see, you mother will be coming to your rescue any minute now" he explained. And the second she sees you stuck in the cage, and realizes that if she did not hand over the last gem, I would kill you" Gethin said, and then shouted the end. Ewald's heart nearly stopped, could his mother let Gethin kill him. It had been a few minutes afterwards, and Ewald was getting scared. In the far distance he could hear the cheers of students and teachers, as they watched the game and celebrated the remaining two weeks that they will have at this school.

Finally a blue flash emitted from the small square transporter, but it was not who Ewald wanted to see. Two men appeared their faces wide with fake smiles. They both had tuxedos, and fancy imported shoes. One wore black rough hair, unlike the other who had curly dark blonde. Official black shades covered half of their face, making them look more secretive. So far Ewald did not like them. He only assumed the worst that they were the only new army that Gethin could raise. The man with the black hair looked down at Ewald with a demining eye; the second man paid no attention. "We need back up" the man screamed into his transceiver, he looked more scared than ever. "Gethin has returned," he added into his microphone. Unlucky for them it was too late, Gethin had picked up his hand and pointed it at them; within second they were on the ground. Ewald screeched, as he stared at their bodies. The trapped boy looked at their chests, it had been declared, and they were dead. Ewald felt like crying, this is worse than any nightmare, in seconds he also could be gone.

The only thing Ewald could hope for was that the back up would soon arrive; he now had decided that if his mother had come it would be worse. Ewald was relieved that his mother had not come, but it was the back up that had come. It again flashed; five more officials appeared as they stepped off again. "So this is your back up" he chuckled insulting their plans. "Why have you returned?" asked a voice that sounded even older than Gethin's. His sapphire eyes disappeared for a few seconds then returned. "It's you" Gethin muttered, unhappy of whom it was. "Remove the cage," the hidden voice commanded of his guards. One of the black suited men centered their magic, through their hands and to the cage. He swung his hands back as it lifted itself and flew behind the trees. Gethin aimed at the man, planning on killing him, but he missed hitting the guard to his left. Ewald picked himself off of the ground and ran back to the transporter. The faster he ran the harder it would be for Gethin to get him, he quickly thought. With a long leap, he landed on the transporter.

He pushed off, scrapping the platform with the bottom of his shoes. He needed to get to safety, Ewald needed to find Alex in the middle of around five hundred students. Surprisingly it did not take a lot of time, Alex's clothing stood out clearly. Alexander was the only person not wearing either blue or red. Ewald jumped up the bleachers to get to him, he walked in front of the students as he tried to enter the middle. Alex noticed his dirty friend running up the steps, automatically he ran down to meet him. "What happened?" he asked very concerned, "Gethin..." Ewald said panting, he was still out of breath from the running. Alexander walked down the steps with him, "You saw him?" He asked really wanting to know. "Yes" Ewald answered making Alex smile, "No, well not really" he tried to explain that he had not seen Gethin's face. "Let's talk about it over there" Alex suggested pointing near the tall rectangular hedge.

They arrived at their chosen destination. Ewald leaned onto the tall green bush; it was surprisingly stable and could hold him up. "So, what happened?" Alex asked, doing the same. "Gethin has two gems, right?" Ewald said, asking his friend just to verify that they all understood that fact. "Well we know that my mom had it, so he tried to capture me" he continued with the story. "And, when your mother would get there he would tell her that it was you or the gem" Alexander interrupted, a large smirk grew over his face, he knew that Ewald would be amazed by him. Ewald waited not wanting to jump to conclusions, "How do you know?" He asked confused. "Isn't it obvious?" He asked holding the suspense, "I'm the one who helped him enter Tralbon." Ewald screamed internally, "You are on Gethin's side?" he asked feeling betrayed. Alexander did not reply, he only kept a clean look on his face. Suddenly his lips began to twitch as it turned into a big smile, "I was only kidding" he joked letting out a huge laugh. His friend did not, "That's not funny" he yelled slightly embarrassed. The two quieted down, "So, you really would believe that I would betray you?" he asked with wonder. "I don't know," he answered not wanting to hurt anybody's feelings.

"Okay so, how did you escape?" Alex asked, "Two officers from the magic section came through the transporter," he answered. "Sadly, they both died" Ewald added. Alex shot a nasty look; he did indeed hate hearing about deaths, and blood. "Then five more came, but there was also another man" he told his friend, "It was someone that Gethin knew," he added, giving more information. Alex thought, "Well, he has many enemies" he clarified. "You never know who it is" Ewald confirmed his very thought. The two said nothing, only the sweet sound of birds and happy cheers bounced onto their eardrums. With a twitch in the air, clouds formed as if ash from an exploding volcano. The wind picked up from barely any to a fake tornado. In an instant Ewald knew what this was, the same wind and clouds from the day he left for Drolers. After that exact thought it began to rain, large water droplets fell over the school. It was even beginning to emit a weird rhythm; luckily right before the rain the referee blew the last whistle. Happiness poured into Alex's heart like thick pure chocolate, as he heard the screams of Selvins. They held up their best player cheering with joy that they had won. "We better head inside" Alex suggested, slightly worried.

"I need you two to follow me," said a voice, they were certain that it was the same person that had placed his hands on their shoulders. They turned around, scared that it might be Gethin. Instead they found their old history teacher; Professor Henderson. He turned wanting them to follow him, as they had no obvious choice they did as told. He led them awkwardly into the two hedges through the petite opening. The teacher looked back at them as he stopped. "I have been told that you know about the gems of time," he said, as it continued to rain. Ewald felt, as he should not answer, "Why" he asked afraid that their professor would turn out to be friends with Gethin. "Oh, just because I have a warning" he answered, "Gethin is not dead" he paused for suspense. Alexander frowned, not because he had found out that he hadn't died, but for the fact that he had gotten away. "He has escaped, the president of the magic section and his guards tried their hardest" he moved on into the storyline. "The only reason I am telling you this is because he does have tricks" Professor Henderson said, "He can have you fooled, set up traps, spies even" added he. Ewald looked over at Alex, "He will do anything for those gems; he doesn't care for anyone or anything but himself" he described. By the second Gethin sounded worse and worse to the boys. "So here is my advice, don't trust anyone" the teacher said in a snappy voice. He stared at Alex for a few seconds then turned around, and walked up the stairs.

"That was helpful" Alexander commented about the teacher's short speech. To Ewald's ears it sounded slightly sarcastic, but Alex meant it truly. "Let's get inside before we become even more wet" Ewald suggested helpfully, although it was slightly impossible as they were completely covered from head to toe in water. Alexander shook himself like a large hound; it shot amounts of rain towards Ewald. He wasn't too grateful but they would be dry in a few minutes. Together they walked indoors and ended their day peacefully.

Chapter 17

Something Mysterious

Two weeks had passed since the day that Ewald had met Gethin. The Katnors were still depressed that they hadn't won, but they had other priorities. The school was filling themselves with piles of studying; day after day they would be introduced to a new test. It was the last day in fact, and they were finishing up their last test.

Alex wrote the final answer on the piece of paper, this was the easiest test that he had ever written. He stood up with a smile as he walked between the desks towards the front. Alexander felt like laughing, his first time in potions class to beat everyone to finishing was now. Professor Hegnorf looked up not really surprised that Alex had finished before everybody else. Even Dhiman Letap was struggling. "Thank You" he thanked him as he grabbed the last test of the year. Three minutes later the final bell rung and the remaining students rushed, scribbling over the answers. Ewald walked up to Alex who was leaving the room. "Hey, so how was it?" he asked, "I think I aced it" he answered with confidence. Ewald smiled, "That was the best test ever," Alex added. "Wow first time you ever said that about a... test" he remarked. He only shrugged to that comment. The group of students turned into the sorting room, "Wait where are we going?" Alex asked finally noticing that they were blindly moving. Ewald didn't answer, as he didn't know. "Hello, I'm Julie" she reminded them from the front of the room. "Now if you may recall, I lead you to Tralbon" she reminded Alexander who was absent minded about her existence. "As tradition I will be leading you out, so if you may follow me" Julie said as she walked out of the room and back through the north tunnel. The students felt no reason to not follow her. They walked down the east tower and through the silver entrance.

The rest of the classes were already at the entrance in large groups of cluttered students. "Time to get onto the buses" she said, as she pointed to the seven buses in front of them. The yellow buses were lined up after each other; they were absent of wings, which must have not yet been activated. All of the buses opened their doors as the crowds jumped at them; they quickly pushed throbbing back and forth. Ewald and Alex shoved themselves in, as they sat down on the rubbery grey seats. It was actually the exact seat that they had sat in before. More students poured in as the seats quickly filled. Dhiman flew in as a muscular girl pushed him in. He sat on the seat next to Alexander, who automatically frowned the second he saw his face. "If you ask me Julie isn't fit to lead us," he inconsiderately said, "A girl with the same age as us, who says they can trust her." "Well nobody asked you" Alex replied with a harsh and cold voice. Ewald looked at Dhiman and smiled, their fights were really getting annoying. With a sudden shake the bus expanded, as more students poured in like a thick pure chocolate.

After all the students had entered the door closed as the buses ahead flew away. Their bus drove a few meters before it flew into the air. 'This is it'

Ewald thought, 'Goodbye Tralbon'. The bus flew off and turned the opposite way, Ewald looked down through the window to see the teachers waving up high. It had been a lengthy journey, but at last the bus began to slow down until it had fully stopped. With a gentle sway it softly fell down to the ground. Alex held onto the seat in front of them, from the scare. The door opened as Julie jumped off first. The rest followed, even thought Dhiman think it not wise.

Julie pulled out the pink powder from her belt, as everyone finished exiting the silent bus. She flicked it out of her palm; a large entrance dug itself into the wall. A long path appeared which lead inside. Alex looked; from here he could see the now empty eating area. Together the packs of people walked in like a cool gang. The white bricks of Drolers felt blindingly white before they got used to them. The hospital was empty, only one woman stood. Her thick body moving back and forth as she cleaned the floor with a long broom. Her pale face not even noticing them, she continued to keep her head bowed down. The students moved slower and slower as they stared at her. A tall thin man walked up to her, he kept his face hidden from the boys and girls. Silently he leaned inwards and whispered to her, keeping his over tanned hand over his small mouth. Then with a slow move he backed away, and vanished. He left her mouth wide open, she was definitely in shock. The old lady dropped her broom onto the ground, and walked towards Julie. She did just the same as the man, leaning in closely and talking a shocking tale. The same reaction appeared just less intense. She shook her head trying to erase what she had heard, as the old woman went back to sweeping the clean ground.

The group quickened their walking, some had schedules to maintain. "I'm telling you that was about the gems" Alexander said to Ewald, "But they're safe" he replied. Alex looked at him with a strange eye, "They're never safe," he said. They turned left an entered the hospital bedroom. The young teenagers walked into the first room, which they had first appeared into. Alex looked back at the archway, as he shook Ewald. "What?" he asked not as happy as he was before, "Oh" he said. The empty spot on the wall was saddening; it reminded the two of the horrible murder that roamed the outside world. They continued staring at it as they remembered all the trouble that they had gone through to protect the Gems of Time. "Something bad is happening, I can feel it" Alexander informed his friend. "Me and Professor Samantha will be going around to each one of you and transporting you," she announced to the group as she pointed at the professor to her left. Julie looked at them waiting for them to jump onto the beds, "Well, lie down" she commanded.

They all ran to each side of the room and laid

down on the closest bed to them. Ewald was to the left of Alexander. Unluckily they had chosen the second closest bed to Julie, which meant that they had less time to talk. Suzy had been in fact to the left of Ewald. He watched as Julie looked down at the parchment, and pointed the transporter wand at her. A light blue light emitted to Ewald's left, "I'll see you next year" he reassured his friend. "Bye" he said as Julie approached, she pointed her wand directly at his face. "Yeah" Alexander said in a sad voice, a few seconds before he vanished. "Bye" he said, but he was too late. That was it, he won't see his friend for another four months and the last word he had said was "Yeah." Alexander felt ashamed that Ewald hadn't heard his goodbye, but there was no time. Julie looked at him with a concerned look, as if she had seen someone she despised. She swung her wand nearly poking his eye, and then he vanished.

Chapter 18

A Surprise in the Park

The blue light disappeared as the basement replaced the image of Drolers. It had been the first time he had re- entered the cold and barren basement since the beginning of the year. A long smile was scheduled right now, but he had to see his mother safe. Ewald ran up the steps, skipping a few. "Mom" he called, as he saw his new house. The new layers of paint felt as smooth as metal, and the furniture matched. Nothing in the house was the same, except some basic walls. A long sigh of relief spread, Gethin hadn't yet come, but he still didn't see his mother. "Mom" he said more worried, as he ran to every room. She was still not to be found.

Ewald had searched everywhere, by the second he imagined Gethin capturing his mother until she told him the location of the gem. He stood at the front of the door and thought. Only one last thought came to his mind. He opened the closet grabbed a nice sweater, and ran out.

He jogged in pace, this was his last hope. She was the last person he had in his life, he couldn't lose her. As he turned around the corner he held his breath. He caught sight of the green old oak tree, and behind it sat another new tree. Which had grown several flowers, it was a white blossom. He kept running in hope of seeing his mother on the bench. He slowed down of relief; she was peacefully sitting and staring at the tree.

Mrs. Ellington heard the faint sound of footsteps, which were loud enough to hear because no one except for them was present. "Mom" he said as Ewald stumbled over his feet and landed in her arms. "Ewald" she replied as she hugged him, "I'm so glad you're safe." "Mom, I missed you so much" Ewald exclaimed, "I thought he got you" he added sounding concerned as he sat on the cream bench. "Who Gethin?" she asked already knowing the answer, "He's gone," she informed. He was confused, "Wait no he isn't" Ewald told to get her aware. "Oh" she said taking back her words, "At least the Gems of Time are out of his hands" she told. Ewald's mother thought, "And out of ours" she explained making him feel safer.

"I have some questions," Ewald said asking permission. She gently nodded her head, "What happened the day I left for Drolers?" he asked. Mrs. Ellington thought of the best way to explain the story, "That day was the day you had to leave for school, I was nervous and I didn't have enough time to explain what would happen" she told almost apologizing. "Why were you nervous?" Ewald asked, wanting more information. "Well there was a meeting that night, with the other gem holders and minister, and it was at our house. That's why I had cooked a turkey and put three plates around it," she said as she fed him knowledge. "The meeting, what was it for?" he asked not exactly understanding. "It was about the recent news that Gethin had been sighted again," his mother answered. "Mom" Ewald said in a sullen voice, "What was the reason for the sudden clouds, rain, and sound?" "When ever Gethin enters or leaves the area a terrible storm begins," she explained. Ewald paused to think, "But why was he there?" "He was planning on crashing the meeting. He saw it as an opportunity, as he had all gem holders in one place" she explained into more detail, still staring at the oak tree. "Wait, there's one more thing from that night. What was the loud thud on the door?" Ewald asked remembering everything that night. She thought to think back, "The minister was holding off Gethin. They had a long fight, until he left." "Oh" replied Ewald. A long period of silence flew over them, not a sound entered their ears.

"Do you know why that tree had grown?" Mrs. Ellington asked as she signaled towards the white blossom tree. "No" he replied, as she had expected. "A new tree will grow every time Gethin comes out and is defeated," she explained anxiously. Ewald had never thought of that, "Get up" she nicely commanded, and he did just the same. Mrs. Ellington turned around, as she aimed at the bench; it flew into the air, rotated, and fell back down. "There, now we can see both trees" she exclaimed knowing that it would amaze her son. His mouth dropped down, "Mom how did you do that?" "They sent a pamphlet home, to do basic stuff," she informed with a smile. Slowly they sat back down. "That was awesome," he added complementing her even more. "So I was thinking that we have the best summer ever," she said exciting him, right now he felt like he was the only boy in the world. "And, after you can go back to Tralbon" she told him, "And Alexander." "I'm so glad I'm going to Tralbon, not that old dump filled with bullies and lab rats," he said with a chuckle slightly over exaggerating the public school's situation. "I'm glad you're happy" his mother informed him, he smiled of joy. "So, what are we going to do?" he asked anxious for family time. "Just wait," she told him, as she looked at the oak tree with dark green leaves, swaying in the wind.

Be Sure To Catch

The Next Book In The Ewald Series

Coming Out Late 2013/Early 2014

The Ewald Series

ewaldseries.com

Dedicated to

My loving parents

Hanadi and Majdi

About the Illustrator

Hanadi Bader

Hanadi is a talented young artist that excels in depicting the figure and landscapes; the post-impressionists influence her paintings. Her paintings are in numerous private collections. Mrs.Bader participated in many art shows, in addition to eleven sole exhibitions in multiple countries. Hanadi Bader currently lives with her family in Canada.

HanadiBader.com